D0340249

Not What I Expected

Monday, August 18, 4:40 pm

High School Diary

...insisted I eat this...

...by the time Mrs. Montele...

...gs I obviously couldn't say...

...'t eaten the bacon.

...Sinclair." I looked down...

...jeans. I knew I was...

THE MOSTLY MISERABLE LIFE
OF APRIL SINCLAIR

Not What I Expected

LAURIE FRIEDMAN

darbycreek
MINNEAPOLIS

The images in this book are used with the permission of: © Pshonka/Dreamstime.com (pumpkin); iStockphoto.com/PandaWild (smiley face and laughing face).

Darby Creek
A division of Lerner Publishing Group, Inc.
241 First Avenue North
Minneapolis, MN 55401 USA

For reading levels and more information, look up this title at www.lernerbooks.com.

Main body text set in Janson Text LT Std 12/17.
Typeface provided by Linotype AG.

Library of Congress Cataloging-in-Publication Data

Friedman, Laurie B., 1964–
  Not what I expected / by Laurie Friedman.
    pages cm. — (The mostly miserable life of April Sinclair ; #5)
    Summary: "April Sinclair has always looked forward to high school. But with a jealous BFF, fighting parents, and self-doubt about romance, ninth grade may be more than April bargained for"— Provided by publisher.
    ISBN 978-1-4677-8588-4 (lb : alk. paper)
    ISBN 978-1-4677-8829-8 (eb pdf : alk. paper)
    1. High schools—Fiction. 2. Schools—Fiction. 3. Dating (Social customs)—Fiction. 4. Friendship—Fiction. 5. Family life—Fiction. 6. Diaries—Fiction. I. Title.
  PZ7.F89773No 2015
  [Fic]—dc23   2014046272

Manufactured in the United States of America
2 – BP – 11/1/15

For Becca, the best daughter a
mother could ask for

One is not born,

but rather becomes,

a woman.

—*Simone de Beauvoir*

I'm not sure which is more traumatizing—learning how to put in a tampon or teaching your little sister how to do it. Actually, I do know. The experience I just had with May is permanently embedded into my brain in the most unfortunate way. She came into my room just as I was settling into bed to watch a double episode of *Grey's Anatomy*. It was how I'd planned to relax on my last night before starting high school.

One look told me May was upset. I shut my laptop. "Is this about what Amanda said at dinner?" I thought for sure it was going to be. But I was so far off.

"I don't know how to use a tampon."

I shook my head like that was a ridiculous thing to be scared about it, and her case it is. "You don't need to know how to use a tampon. You haven't started your period yet. Have you?"

"No. But what if it starts while I'm at school?"

This wasn't the first time May and I had had this talk. I'd already assured her that even if she did start at school, she wasn't going to bleed out all over Fern Falls Middle School. Still, I remember how scary it was starting middle school and worrying about when you were going to get your period. "What'd I tell you about your first period?" I asked May.

"Not much comes out." It sounded more like a question than a statement.

"Right. So keep a few pads hidden in your backpack and just put one on if you need it."

"But what if my first period is heavy?" asked May. "I've read that it can be."

I glanced at the clock on my nightstand. It was getting later by the minute, and I had a lot of TV to watch. "Everyone I know had a light first period. Don't worry."

I thought I sounded fairly authoritative, but May wasn't convinced. "Did you ask everyone you know if their first period was light?"

I blew a piece of hair off my face in response. Her question sounded annoyingly like something Mom would ask. She ignored my lack of an answer and continued on. "Besides, I don't think I'll be able to play soccer or softball with a pad on."

Since I don't do field sports, it was kind of hard for me to comment on that. "Maybe you need to talk to Mom. It's her job to teach you these sorts of things."

"Mom said she'd teach me at the '*right time*.'" May enunciated the words like her definition of the right time and Mom's weren't the same. Then she looked at me, her big brown eyes popping out from under a fringe of stick-straight bangs. "I need to know. Just in case. Please, April. You're my big sister."

I let out a breath. I knew she wasn't going to leave me alone unless I helped her. Plus, I have to admit that part of me felt sorry for her. "C'mon," I said. I grabbed May by the arm and led her into the bathroom. But before I could shut the door behind us, June followed us in.

"What are y'all doing?" she asked.

"April is teaching me how to use a tampon," said May.

I slapped my head. I couldn't believe May told her what we were doing. She should have known this was NOT an activity that June needed to know anything about.

But it was clearly something June was interested in. "Can I watch?" she asked.

"NO!" I said. Mom would kill me if she knew I was letting my eight-year-old sister witness Tampon Insertion 101.

June put her hand on her hip and made no movement towards the door. "C'mon," she said. "I know what tampons are for. I know all about periods."

June always has a book in her hands and is an emerging smarty (Mom's word, not mine) on lots of topics, but I was surprised this was one of them. I watched open-mouthed as she reached into the cabinet under the sink and took out my box of tampons. "I'll read the directions while you show her what to do," she said.

This had wrong written all over it, but no way was I giving this lesson twice. "Suit yourself," I said.

June grinned victorious, plopped down on the ground, handed May a tampon, pulled the instruction leaflet out of the box, and started reading. "After washing your hands, remove the product from the wrapper and get into a comfortable position sitting on the toilet, squatting slightly with knees bent, or standing with one foot on the toilet seat."

May shot me a look.

"Go with option one," I said.

May washed up, then pulled down her shorts and panties and sat on the toilet. She grinned like she was proud of having completed the first step. I felt vaguely nauseous.

June kept reading. "To insert the applicator, hold the outer insertion tube by the finger grip with your thumb and middle finger. With the removal string hanging down, insert the tip of the applicator at a slight upward angle. Slide the outer insertion tube in until your fingers touch your body."

May stopped grinning. "Eww," she said. "I don't want to do that."

I didn't think I should have to remind May that she's the one who wanted to learn how to use a tampon. "Keep reading," I commanded June.

"To push the tampon inside you, push the inner tube with your pointer finger all the way into the outer tube, or use your other hand to push the inner tube. Remove the inner and outer applicator tubes at the same time. The tampon should now be comfortably inside you, with the removal string hanging outside your body."

May shook her head. "I don't know what any of that means."

"Do you want June to read it again?" I asked.

"No," said May. She held the tampon out towards me. "Can you show me?"

"Just stick it in," I said. I gave May my best you-can-do-it look, but when I did, I saw the tears forming. I racked my brain. "It doesn't hurt. I promise."

May sniffled. "Please."

I looked at the tampon in her hand. It was a light one. "You pick up kids twice your size. For fun. You can put that little thing inside you."

May shifted on the toilet. "I don't pick up kids anymore. I'm going to middle school." A tear rolled down her cheek. "I'm scared."

I took a deep breath. I knew she wasn't talking about putting in the tampon. "Middle school will be fine," I said. "You'll make new friends, you'll get used to switching classes. All the bad things you worry might happen won't. If I survived middle school, you can too. I promise."

When I finished, May blew her nose into a piece of toilet paper. I actually thought we were done. I waited for her to stand and zip up. But that's not what happened.

"Now can you show me how to put this in?" She waved the tampon in front of me.

This was an honor I didn't need or want. But as the saying goes, it was time to get on with the show. Literally. I took a deep breath, unzipped, and then put in a tampon as both my little sisters watched. "See, that wasn't so bad." I wasn't sure if I was saying it to myself or my little sister. Either way, I'd had all I could take. "My work here is done," I said as I left.

I'd much rather watch *Grey's Anatomy* than May's anatomy.

10:42 p.m.
Post-Grey's

Dad just came and told me to turn my light off. "I can't believe my number one daughter is going to high school tomorrow," he said.

That makes two of us. The whole purpose of watching *Grey's* was to help me relax and not think about it, but now it's all I can think about. The dinner we had earlier tonight didn't help. Since we go back to school tomorrow, Dad thought it would be nice to have a family gathering, so all my aunts, uncles, cousins, Gaga, Willy, and Sophie and her mom, Emma, convened at the Love Doctor Diner. As soon as we sat down with our plates of fried chicken, egg salad sandwiches, and Dad's homemade pickled peaches, the back-to-school talk started.

"Charlotte, Izzy, I can't believe you girls are starting first grade," said Gaga. "Are you ready?" she asked.

Charlotte nodded. "I got a Hello Kitty backpack."

"I got a Thomas the Tank Engine lunch box," added Izzy.

My cousin Amanda rolled her eyes. "It's kind of weird for a first-grader to have a Thomas the Tank Engine lunch box," she mumbled.

Aunt Lilly shot her daughter a look. "There's nothing wrong with Thomas. If that's Izzy's choice, you should respect it."

"Sure," said Amanda. Then she took a bite out of a drumstick like she didn't care what kind of lunch box Izzy got.

Gaga continued on around the table. "June, fourth grade is big. I'm sure you will excel academically and watch out for your younger cousins."

"I'll be in third grade," said June.

Gaga ignored the correction and kept going. "May, are you ready for middle school?"

"I guess," said May. But as I watched her shift around in her chair, I could tell she was nervous. I think Gaga could tell too because she looked at Amanda, who dresses and acts like she's sixteen, but is only a year ahead of May in school.

"Amanda, do you have any advice for your younger cousin?"

Amanda smacked her overly glossed lips. "Yep. Don't go in the bathroom by the gym. The seventh and eighth grade girls will beat the crap out of you."

"Amanda!" Aunt Lilly and Uncle Dusty looked furious.

"Please tell your cousin you're kidding," said Uncle Dusty.

Amanda rolled her eyes. "Sure," she said to May. "I'm kidding." Then she started laughing, which made it impossible to tell if she was kidding or not. May looked terrified.

Gaga frowned at Amanda, but then she smiled at Sophie's mom, Emma. "Your dad and I are so happy you and Sophie are here in Faraway with us, Emma, especially with Sophie and April going to school together."

Emma smiled like she's happy too, but I know from Sophie that her mom is having a hard time with the "trial separation" thing and living in Faraway. How could she not? It must be so different from what she's used to in Paris or New York.

Gaga finished what I guess she considered to be her obligatory back-to-school round up with a nod toward my oldest cousin. "Harry, I really can't believe you'll be a junior this year. I'm sure you understand that the decisions you make now will affect the rest of your life."

Aunt Lilly put her hand on her son's shoulder. "With college applications right around the corner, we've talked about how important it is to do well academically. Harry's on board. Right, Harry?"

Harry frowned. I wasn't sure if it was because he was annoyed that his mother was talking about him in this weird third-person way or because he wasn't happy about the added pressure. "Junior year is going to suck," he said.

Aunt Lila looked at her twins and gasped. "I don't like that word," she told them.

"Harry!" Aunt Lilly scolded. "Please don't use that word, and try to be positive." Amanda laughed again.

"I get what he's saying," said Sophie. "It's kind of scary knowing that how you do in school affects where you go to college, and even how your life could turn out." Then she winked at Harry. He looked surprised, and maybe even happy, that she'd come to his rescue.

When dinner was over, everyone said goodnight and we went home. But as we drove, my mind filled with so many thoughts. Big things, like when do the decisions you make and the things you do start to affect the rest of your life? Junior year? Earlier?

Also more personal things, like, will I still be close with Billy and Brynn? They've been my best friends since third grade, but things have changed since they started going out this summer. It's mostly Brynn. She's so possessive of Billy, like he belongs to her or something. I'm not even sure he's aware of it. But it feels weird to me, especially since he and I went out way before he got together with Brynn.

And what will it be like going to school with Sophie? It's surreal that I have an almost-cousin/new best friend in Faraway. It's still weird that her grandfather and Gaga got married, and crazy that she and her mom moved here when her parents decided to separate, and that tomorrow, she's going to Faraway High School with me.

And then there's Matt. Things were so good when we went out last spring, but he was such a jerk this summer for trying to kiss Sophie. I was so upset when I came home from camp, and we broke up. He said we'd see how things are when school starts. It's not even like I want to get back together with him. I'm pretty much over it now. But it doesn't help that he lives next door. I just have no idea what it's going to be like when I see him at school or on the street. I don't really know what anything will be like.

As I was leaving the diner, Sophie looped an arm through mine and said, "High school here we come!" Like we're going on some exciting adventure.

High school is a new beginning, right? So it should be exciting. But I feel unprepared. I wish there was something simple I could do to feel ready. I have exactly eight hours and forty-two minutes to sleep, wake, shower, flatiron my hair, put on makeup, pick out the perfect first-day outfit, and eat breakfast before getting to school by the time the first bell rings tomorrow. I kind of doubt straight hair is all I'm missing, but I'm out of time for anything else.

Sophie's words echo in my brain. High school here we come.

Ready or not.

Hi. I'm Elle Woods and

this is Bruiser Woods.

We're both Gemini vegetarians.

—*Elle Woods*, Legally Blonde

Monday, August 18, 4:30 p.m.
High School, Day 1
Bottom Line: Uneventful

I can't help that part of me was hoping high school would start and somehow it would be fabulous. I don't know what I was hoping for. Hot guys? No homework? Low-cal snacks? But it wasn't anything like that. At least for me.

My day started in Mrs. Monteleone's homeroom. She asked us to go around the room and introduce ourselves and tell the class something we'd like everyone to know. Even though I went to middle school with half the kids in my homeroom, I still wanted to lead with something interesting. But I couldn't think of one interesting thing to say about myself that wasn't weird.

Things that came to mind: (1) my dog's name is Gilligan (weird), (2) my dad owns the Love Doctor Diner downtown, which makes the best pecan pies and Key lime pies around (also weird), and (3) until last year, my boobs were two different sizes (very weird).

But as I was thinking, my stomach started rumbling (probably from the bacon and eggs Mom insisted I eat this morning), which was completely distracting, and by the time Mrs. Monteleone got to me, I'd only thought about things I obviously couldn't say about myself and how much I wished I hadn't eaten the bacon.

"Um, my name is April Sinclair." I looked down and picked a fleck of dirt off my freshly washed jeans. I knew I wasn't being interesting. "I'm on the dance team." Slightly more interesting. "And I'm really excited about high school." Ugh. Uninteresting, bordering on pathetic. That was enough. I looked at Mrs. Monteleone and pressed my lips together like I was done.

Fortunately, she picked up on my cue. "Thank you, April. I'm excited you're here too."

I ignored a stray giggle coming from the back of the classroom and focused on Mrs. Monteleone's chin. From where I was sitting, it looked like there was a hair sprouting out of it, which I later confirmed with Julia Lozano, who has Mrs. Monteleone for second period history, is in fact the case. Writing that makes me feel pathetic, like noticing my homeroom teacher's chin hair was the most interesting thing that happened to me today.

The rest of my day was just so very predictable. I found out who's in all my classes. I have bio with Sophie. Algebra with Brynn. English with Sophie and Billy. History with Emily. I ate lunch. I was assigned a locker. I got my student ID card.

Nothing bad happened, but nothing good happened either. Everything fell into the nonmemorable shade of gray category, even the picture on my ID, which did nothing to highlight my soft skin or naturally good-smelling breath and made my bad features (misshapen nose/hair that tends to frizz) look worse than usual. The day made me feel very mediocre, especially in contrast to Sophie. As we walked home after school, she was literally brimming with excitement. "I love Faraway High," she said.

I didn't see how that could be possible. I know Sophie is a glass-half-full kind of girl, but honestly, she went to an art school in New York, and before that, an American School in Paris that was filled with kids of foreign diplomats. This had to pale in comparison. "What did you like best?" I asked. "The wilted lettuce on the salad bar or the unairconditioned bio lab?"

Sophie frowned like she disapproved of my sarcasm. "I liked a lot of things, but what I liked best was that everyone was so friendly."

I actually laughed when she said that. "Really?"

Sophie paused and looked at me like what she was about to say was for my benefit. "It's a new year. New things can happen. You have to stay open to the possibilities."

"Sure," I said. And I intend to. But that's easier said than done, and much easier for Sophie than for me. She just has this way about her. The world and everyone in it (including me) likes her. Though sometimes her optimism gets on my nerves.

Like today.

Thursday, August 21, 6:18 p.m.
Everyone likes Sophie

She's definitely the new *it* girl at Faraway High School. Part of it is that she's from New York and Paris, which makes her cool. Plus, with her long dark hair and pale skin, she's pretty in a unique way, which doesn't hurt. But I think the reason she's so popular is because she's nice to everyone. Even weird people like Katia Sommers and Harry.

I've gone to school with Katia my entire life, and we've never spoken a word to each other. That makes me sound snotty, but it's not the case. Katia always made it clear she didn't want anyone to talk to her. She might as well have worn a T-shirt that said: *One word and I'll deck you.* All through middle school, she sat alone at lunch or assemblies, and if anybody got within a foot of her, she literally growled like a rabid dog that might bite. All week she showed up to school in full Goth black, which made her seem less approachable than ever.

But apparently, not to Sophie. "Can we sit here?" Sophie asked Katia Tuesday at lunch. Without waiting for an answer, she plopped down next to Katia with her tray and looked at me like I should too. "You're in my art class," said Sophie.

Katia glared in return, but Sophie seemed oblivious as she chatted on about oils and inks. Surprisingly, Katia relaxed into the conversation, and the three of us have been lunch buddies all week. Today, we took a fourth into our group. Harry was walking by our table with a tray and looking around like he had nowhere to go, and Sophie said, "Sit with us."

Harry stood there. I could tell he was too shocked to move. I'm sure he was thinking that it would be weird for him to eat lunch with a brunch of freshman girls, but Sophie scooted over and patted the empty seat next to her like she'd made room and it would be rude if Harry didn't sit. Honestly, I think he was relieved Sophie invited him to join us.

Then she started talking about music. In the short time she's gotten to know Harry, I know she's figured out that music is one of the few topics he actually likes to talk about. Harry talked for an uncharacteristically long time about a new band from Ireland that he really likes. We all thought they sounded cool, and Sophie said, "Why don't we all get together this weekend. We can hang out and listen to their music."

So we made a plan, and that's what we're doing on Sunday, which is kind of weird because (a) Harry has been my cousin my whole life, and I've never hung out with him except at family gatherings, and (b) I've also never hung out with (or even spoken to) Katia and now we eat lunch together every day and we're doing something this weekend.

It's not that I have a problem with it. Actually, I think it's cool. It's just weird, because Sophie showed up and brought people together in a way that wouldn't have happened if she hadn't been here, and everyone but Sophie knows that's the case. It's like she forgot to pick up her copy of the Faraway rule book.

Friday, August 22, 6:08 p.m.

I invited Billy, Brynn, and Sophie to come over after school today. That sounds so grade-school playdate-ish, but I wanted to start the year off doing something with Brynn *and* Billy, and I wanted them to get to know Sophie. When she moved here, everyone was busy getting ready for school, and we hadn't really had a chance to all hang out together.

But it didn't turn out like I'd hoped. When we went to my room, Billy picked up the jar of lake water that he brought me back from camp two summers ago when my parents wouldn't let me go. "I can't believe you still have this." He laughed, I think at the memory of when he gave it to me, which was when he asked me to go out.

I laughed too. "I'd never get rid of a jar of Camp Silver Shores water," I said.

"That's gross," said Brynn. Then she plopped down on the floor and patted the space next to her. "Sit here," she said to Billy. He did, but I think he only did it because it would seem like a big deal if he hadn't. There was an uncomfortable silence.

Billy finally broke it. "So how are you doing with your parents' separation?" he asked Sophie.

Brynn shot him a look. "I'm sure she doesn't want to talk about that." Then she changed the subject and started talking about how hard her locker is to open.

"I actually don't mind talking about it," Sophie said to Brynn. "My parents are just going through a trial separation. It's not a big deal."

But I knew it was a bigger deal to Sophie than she was letting on, and I think Billy knew it too. "It must be hard," he said.

"It is," acknowledged Sophie. "My dad is in Paris. I miss him a lot." Then she smiled at Billy. "Thanks for asking me about it. I guess I haven't really talked about it much."

Billy smiled at her. "Glad I could help."

I looked at Brynn as she bit off a cuticle. She only does that when she's nervous. Billy might have been glad he could help Sophie, but it was pretty clear Brynn wasn't.

Sunday, August 24, 9:17 p.m.
In my room
Off the phone
Finally

My ear hurts, which I guess isn't surprising since I spent the last two hours on the phone.

First, I talked to Harry. He, Sophie, Katia and I all hung out today. When they came over, I thought they'd stay maybe an hour, but one turned into five. We listened to music and then took a personality profile test we found online. At first, I was kind of upset with the results. Sophie was classified as an Idealist. Harry and Katia were both Artists, and I was a Duty Fulfiller.

"That's such a boring thing to be," I said when Sophie read the results.

"Not at all," said Sophie. "Duty Fulfillers are loyal, faithful, and honest. Everyone likes being friends with people like that."

"That's true," said Katia, even though (a) I'm not sure she's ever had a friend (from any category), and (b) I'm not entirely convinced I'm a Duty Fulfiller. But Harry agreed, which made me feel better about my classification, so I decided not to question it. We had a good time as we put other people we know into the personality categories.

Anyway, Harry was just calling to ask if he'd left his sunglasses in my room.

The next call came from Billy, who wanted to see how school is going so far. "I want a full report," he said. It was really cool that he called, and it was fun to catch up. We talked for a long time about school and classes and teachers we like, and which ones we don't. Then he told me he's going to run for one of the two Student Government Association class rep positions.

"I'm sure you'll win," I said. It would be impossible for him not to. He was president at the middle school and widely known as being super responsible. Everyone will vote for Billy.

Then Brynn called. "I'm so nervous for dance team tryouts," she said.

I knew this was a super-sensitive topic, since I made the team last year and she didn't. "You'll make it," I said. "You're a really good dancer, and I'll be there to cheer you on."

"Right," said Brynn. "I mean, I know I'm a good dancer. It's just the whole tryout thing has me a little freaked." Whenever Brynn's anxious, she acts like she's more confident than she really is, so I let her comment go. I know it was just her way of making herself feel better. "You'll do great," I said.

Then Brynn switched the subject. "I'll tell you a secret if you promise not to tell." She cleared her throat like she was about to deliver some big news. "Billy is running for SGA."

"Wow," I said like it was news to me. I didn't think I should tell Brynn that it wasn't.

The last call I got tonight was from Sophie. "I want to get involved in something at school," she said.

"You could go out for the dance team. Tryouts are this week."

Sophie laughed. "You know I'm a terrible dancer."

"How about Art League or Habitat for Humanity? Or you could join the French club." They all seemed like good fits for her.

"Maybe," said Sophie, like she was considering my suggestions. "I'm just not sure what I want to do."

"I'm sure you'll figure it out," I said.

Sophie laughed again. "If I don't, I'll just pick something. It would be cool to do something new and totally random."

It was such a Sophie thing to say.

You can tell how smart people are by what they laugh at.

—*Tina Fey*

Wednesday, August 27, 6:32 p.m.
Post-tryouts
Post-smoothies

Dance tryouts were this afternoon, and Brynn made it. Since the beginning of middle school, we've talked about how much fun it would be to be on the team together, and I know how much she wanted it. But she did something this afternoon that makes it hard to be totally happy for her.

I was in the gym with the rest of the team and the girls who were trying out. There were a few other kids in the gym who had come to give moral support. Everyone was hanging out, waiting for Ms. Baumann to start tryouts, when Sophie showed up.

I was talking to Brynn and Emily and another girl on the team, Kate. Sophie spotted us and came over to our group. "I came to wish you luck," she said to Brynn, smiling.

"Thanks," said Brynn in a clipped voice. Then she turned her back to Sophie and kept talking to Emily and Kate like she didn't care if Sophie had come or not. Sophie pursed her lips. I could tell she was trying to decide what to make of Brynn's reaction.

When Ms. Baumann started tryouts, she asked anyone not trying out to leave, and Sophie did. But as Ms. Baumann broke the girls into groups and had them dance, I was still thinking about what had happened. It was sweet of Sophie to come and kind of cold of Brynn to not be more appreciative.

Then, when Ms. Baumann finally announced who made the team, there was lots of screaming and hugging. I gave Brynn a big hug and so did Emily and Kate. "We should stop for smoothies on the way home," Emily said to Brynn as the gym started to clear out.

"Perfect!" said Emily.

"It'll be a celebration!" I said, smiling at Brynn and trying to keep the mood light. But when we got our smoothies and sat down, I said something to Brynn about what happened. "That was sweet of Sophie to come to wish you luck," I said.

"Um, I guess," she said. Then Brynn gave me a blank look almost like she didn't know what I was talking about.

But I knew she knew exactly what I was talking about, and as we walked, I couldn't look at her. She'd been mean to Sophie, plus she was hanging on Emily's every word and laughing at all her jokes. Last year when I'd made the team and she hadn't, she told me she didn't like or trust Emily. Now, she's acting like Emily is her new best friend and Sophie is her number one enemy.

I don't get it. Or her.

9:42 p.m.
Still trying to get it

Aside from doing my algebra homework, I've been spending most of the night trying to figure out why Brynn acted the way she did today. It was nice of Sophie to go to tryouts. She was clearly there to support Brynn. So why was Brynn so rude to her?

Is she jealous that I have a new friend? Did she feel threatened when Billy asked Sophie about her parent's separation? Does she just not like her? I don't know what her problem is, but I have to get to the bottom of it because two of my best friends can't not like each other.

Can they?

10:05 p.m.

I thought about calling Brynn and talking to her about how she treated Sophie, but Billy called to say hi and I decided to talk to him instead. "I wouldn't read much into it. She was probably just nervous about tryouts," he said when I told him what I happened.

I should have known Billy would defend Brynn. "That's probably it," I said. But I wasn't convinced.

When I hung up with Billy, I called Sophie. I wanted to make sure she wasn't upset. But when I brought up what happened, all she said was that it was no big deal and that I shouldn't be worried about it because she's not.

Sophie is always honest, but I had a feeling this time was an exception to the rule.

Thursday, August 27, 9:45 p.m.
Supposed to be studying for bio test
Brain elsewhere

This afternoon I asked Sophie if she wanted to come over to study together for our bio test tomorrow, but her head was clearly somewhere else, because the way she answered was, "I decided I'm going to run for SGA."

"Student Government Association?"

Sophie laughed. "That's what it stands for." She waited. "You don't think it's a good idea?"

"I'm not sure," I said honestly.

"I know it will be hard to win," said Sophie.

"There are only two freshman spots, and I don't know who all is going to run. Plus, I'm the new girl. It's not like everybody knows me yet. But I really want to do this. Even if I don't win, I'll meet a lot of people." She paused for me to take in her reasoning. "There's a meeting next week for anyone who wants to run. I'm going to sign up. I think it's a good idea."

"Me too," I said encouragingly. Sophie should try if that's what she wants to do. She's new and that makes her a long shot to win, although if anyone can do it, she can.

But as Sophie chatted on, I couldn't help thinking about what Brynn's reaction will be when she hears Sophie is doing the same thing as Billy. She should be cool with it, but she's weirdly territorial about Billy. It shouldn't be a big deal.

I don't think it will be. Unless Sophie wins.

Tuesday, September 2, 7:09 p.m.

Tonight when I was walking Gilligan, I saw Matt walking Matilda. "What's up?" he asked as he walked toward me.

How was I supposed to answer that question? I hadn't spoken to him since late July, when we broke up. "Not much." I hoped my voice sounded neutral.

He ran a hand through his hair. "How do you like high school?"

"Good." I appreciated that he was asking, but mostly, I just wanted to go back into my house.

"How's dance?" Three questions. For Matt, that was a record.

I told him that our first competition was at the end of the month, and then we were performing at Homecoming in October and had the dance show in November.

"Cool," he said when I finished. Then he laughed, at what I don't know. I didn't think anything I'd just told him was humorous.

Maybe he was stalling, waiting for me to ask how he was doing, but I didn't. The words just wouldn't come out of my mouth.

"See ya," he said, like bumping into each other was no big deal.

"See ya," I said like it was no big deal for me

either. And surprisingly, it wasn't. I thought it would be weird or uncomfortable seeing him, but it wasn't as bad as I thought it would be. End of story.

I don't even know why I'm writing about it.

You never really understand a person until you consider things from his point of view . . . . Until you climb inside of his skin and walk around in it.

—*Harper Lee*, To Kill a Mockingbird

Thursday, September 11, 7:45 p.m.
I hate politics

Everyone I know is obsessed with the SGA race. The elections are tomorrow, and it's pretty much the only thing anyone has been talking about all week. At least the people I know.

Sophie has been talking about it nonstop. Ever since she signed up to run, she's been on a campaign to meet everyone in our class, which isn't an easy thing to do since there are 337 freshman. All week long she has been passing out campaign stickers that look like lottery tickets with the slogan: Take a chance on the new girl.

Today was the first time all week she stopped to eat lunch instead of just grabbing a snack on her way to fifth period. "What do you think my chances are?" she asked Katia, Harry, and me as she sat down at the table with us.

"You're gonna win," said Katia. I'm not surprised she said that. She and Sophie are in art together, and they have a whole group of friends who already promised they'd vote for Sophie.

Harry agreed. "Most of the kids who are running are losers or freaks."

Sophie laughed. "You hardly know them."

"I don't want to know them," said Harry.

Sophie ignored Harry's cynicism and looked at me. "April, what do you think?"

The truth was that there was no way to know who would win. Billy would definitely get one spot, but there are six kids running for two spots. I'd like to believe a girl would get the other spot, and since three are running, I think Sophie's chances are probably equal to theirs. "You could definitely win," I said.

Sophie sighed. "That sounds like a diplomatic way of saying I might not."

I felt bad that Sophie thought I doubted her. I think she could tell what I was thinking because she laughed. "I'll forgive you as long as you promise to pass out campaign stickers for me tomorrow morning," she said.

"Deal," I said, even though I'd already told Billy I'd pass out stickers for him too.

I wasn't the only one campaigning for him. Brynn had become his self-appointed campaign manager, and she was being very aggressive in her efforts to get him elected.

During our break at dance, Brynn was trying to rally support for him. "Vote for Billy Weiss tomorrow," she told all the freshman on the team. Then she passed out stickers she'd made with a picture of him when he was a toddler. "He's the cutest candidate running," she said. "But then I'm biased."

She seemed preoccupied with what she was doing, which was why I was caught off guard when she said to me, "Don't you think it's a little weird that Sophie is running for SGA?"

It was the reaction I'd been dreading. I'd had a bad feeling Brynn was going to make this into a bigger deal than it should be. I felt myself getting defensive on Sophie's behalf. "What's weird about it?" I asked.

Brynn shrugged. "It just doesn't seem authentic." She looked at Emily who was standing next to her. "We're on the dance team because we're really into dance."

Emily nodded like that made sense.

That was all the validation Brynn needed to continue. "Why does Sophie want to get involved in student government? I have a hard time imagining her doing student government at her art school in New York. They probably didn't even have it at her school in Paris. So why do you think she wants to do it now?"

Brynn looked at me like she was on the debate team and she'd made her argument now it was my turn to rebut.

But luckily, Ms. Baumann called us back to practice at that exact moment.

I didn't want to argue with Brynn. Sophie has a right to do whatever she wants to do. I knew Brynn was implying that Sophie is only doing it because she wants to be with Billy, which I honestly don't think is the case. I also knew that by defending Sophie it would make what Brynn was thinking more valid.

So I didn't.

10:52 p.m.
Don't like what's happening behind closed doors

Sophie has called ten times (OK, four, but it feels like ten) to read me her speech and to talk about what she's going to wear to the assembly tomorrow. But it's hard to focus on what will happen in the school election when I have much more pressing issues at home.

I couldn't help but overhear the conversation Mom and Dad have been having in their room. Their voices were elevated, which is usually a sign they're talking about something worth hearing. Their room is across the hall from mine, and I've been listening undetected outside their door for years. I usually like being in the know, but I wish I hadn't heard the conversation tonight.

"I think opening a downtown boutique is a great idea," Mom said.

"I don't think it's a bad idea." Dad's voice sounded argumentative. "I know you're a talented designer. I just think the timing of opening a new store is wrong." I listened as he talked about the fact that he just recently opened the Love Doctor Diner and how hard it would be on our family if they were both putting in the time required to ensure that a new business is successful. "Flora, it's also a tremendous financial commitment."

I thought what he said made sense and that Mom would agree, but she didn't.

"I've put a lot of time into my business plan," said Mom. She explained how the space she found was a boutique, so all she needs to do is paint and decorate it. "I've already done most of the design work, so the biggest time commitment will be sewing the clothes, and I'm going to hire someone to help me."

"Flora, do you know expensive it is to hire someone?"

Apparently, Mom did. I heard the rustling of papers as she explained to Dad how much it would cost and how she'd finance it.

Honestly, I thought Mom made some good points too. She sounded smart and informed, like she'd done her homework. But as she described her vision for Flora's Fashions to Dad, I started to feel queasy. She's made a lot of my clothes over the years, most of which I found pretty embarrassing to wear. I'm not a big fan of what she's designed, so I was having a hard time imagining other people would be either. But most older ladies, at least the ones in Faraway, have bad taste in clothes. Maybe they'd like her stuff. I just don't know.

But what I do know is that as their conversation shifted from Mom's financial plan to her family plan, I liked it less and less. When Dad asked how she sees the two of them being able to manage things at home, she said that everyone in our family, including him, will need to pitch in and take more responsibility.

I wasn't sure what she had in mind for me. Cleaning toilets? Mowing the yard?

It's not like I don't help out. I'm constantly babysitting my sisters and walking the dog. I've even been pretty good lately about keeping my room clean.

As I crouched outside their door, I waited for Mom to expand on what she meant, but she didn't. "Rex, you're living your dream. Shouldn't I get to live mine?"

"I think it's hard for two people to live their dream at the same time," said Dad.

There was a long silence before Mom responded. "I'm doing this," she said to my dad. "With or without you."

Winning isn't everything,

it's the only thing.

—*Vince Lombardi*

Friday, September 12, 9:29 p.m.
Winners and Losers

Today was a day of winners and losers in Faraway.

This morning was the SGA assembly and election. Billy was a winner. But everyone knew he would be. And Sophie was a winner too!

Everyone seemed to like her new girl platform. She was so poised and sounded so passionate when she talked about giving everyone, even the new girl, a chance. I think people really connected with what she had to say.

She really killed it in her speech, plus she rocked a retro '70s look. And she was so enthusiastic. When she found out she'd won, she was thanking everybody, even though she didn't know who had voted for her.

Emily was also a winner today. At dance practice, Ms. Baumann announced who she had chosen to perform the grade solos at the dance show in November, and she picked Emily to dance the ninth grade solo.

Not that Emily was surprised—she's clearly the best dancer in our grade and one of the best dancers on our team. But still, when she found out, she was so happy. She even hugged Ms. Baumann.

May was a winner too. She played in her first middle school soccer game and scored two goals. She told me all about it the second I got home from dance practice. She's been playing sports for years, and her teams have won lots of games, but I've never seen her so excited.

Mom was also a winner. Tonight at dinner she announced that she signed a lease to rent retail space and that she's opening Flora's

Fashions in downtown Faraway—next month. Even though I knew it was happening, I was surprised it would happen so soon. She showed us the designs she'd drawn and the bolts of fabrics she ordered. She had tears in her eyes, and I wasn't sure what to say when she told us her lifelong dream of opening a store with clothes she designed is finally coming true.

Now for the losers. Or, at least, the people who seem like they've lost something.

First, Brynn. I was standing by her when the SGA winners were announced. When Sophie heard she won, she gave me an excited hug. Then she went to hug Brynn, but Brynn actually pulled away like she didn't want to be hugged by Sophie. Sophie shrugged it off and went right on hugging other people.

Sophie might have been able to let it go, but I couldn't. I felt anger bubbling up inside me. "That was mean." I mumbled the words, but I'd meant for Brynn to hear me, and she had.

She looked at me like she was going to say something in response, but she didn't. "I have to find Billy," she said. Then she ran off, and I watched as she found him and gave him a huge hug. She stayed glued to his side like he was the president and she was the first lady and they were at some official function where they were supposed to stick together.

I looked at Billy to see if he was uncomfortable with it, but it was hard to tell. He was laughing and smiling. I think he was just happy he'd won. But as Billy talked to people, I watched Brynn. I saw her eyes wander across the crowd and settle on Sophie. It was clear she's not happy Billy and Sophie are on SGA together.

Next, my dog. Gilligan had to have his teeth cleaned today, and he had to be knocked out. I didn't even know dogs could have their teeth cleaned. Apparently, Gilligan really needed it, which isn't completely surprising because he has terrible breath. Still, it seemed kind of extreme that a dog would be knocked out for the sake of oral hygiene.

Last, but not least, Dad was a loser. Or at least I could tell he thought he was.

Dad loves to eat, but when Mom announced the news about signing a lease, I watched him pick at his dinner. I think he was worried about how much it's going to cost and where we're going to get the money. I could tell he was scared.

Which actually scared me.

What if something bad happens to my family? What if we run out of money? Thinking about it made me so overwhelmingly tense and stressed that I felt like I had to do something.

So after dinner, I went to my room, locked the door, and broke open the piggy bank I've had since grade school. I literally cracked open my beloved porcelain pig with a hairbrush. I pushed aside the shards and counted up what was inside. It amounted to a whopping $34.79. That's it. I even counted twice. I don't even see how it's possible since I've been depositing all my spare change in there for years.

I wish I could do something helpful. I just don't see any meaningful way if my life savings

is next to nothing, which is why (unfortunately)
I'm putting my name where it belongs.

In the Losers column.

I hope you understand, I'm too tense to pretend I like you.

—*Marge Simpson*

Wednesday, September 17
Study Hall

This morning before school was the first SGA meeting. Not like that should be a big deal for me, when I'm not even on SGA. But I was at my locker getting my books with Brynn when we saw the SGA kids coming out of their meeting. Brynn and I watched as Sophie and Billy walked together from the meeting. They didn't see us see them as they were talking and laughing.

Brynn stiffened.

"I'm sure whatever they're laughing about is no big deal," I said.

But my words, which I'd meant to be calming, had the opposite effect on Brynn. "God," she said. "You always take her side." Then she walked off.

I feel like I need to do something before this situation gets really out of hand.

Friday, September 19, 7:30 p.m.
Talked to Brynn

After dance practice, I asked Brynn if she wanted to go for smoothies. "Great," she said. "Let's see if Emily, Kate, and Vanessa want to go too."

"I'd rather just go with you. I kind of want to talk." I'd been thinking about what I wanted to say since the other day when Brynn had gotten upset about Sophie and Billy laughing together.

"Sure," said Brynn, like it wasn't a problem.

We got our bags and walked to Smoothie King. As we walked, I did the talking. I made the speech I'd carefully rehearsed in my head all day. "I know things have been a little weird since Sophie moved here."

Brynn nodded and looked like she appreciated me acknowledging it.

I kept going. "Even though Sophie moved here and she's kind of family, it doesn't change our friendship." I purposely avoided saying anything accusatory, like pointing out that Brynn had been dismissive to Sophie the day of dance tryouts and downright rude after the SGA election.

"Thanks," said Brynn. "I'm sorry if I've been . . ." She paused like she was trying to find the right word. Then she shrugged and looked down. "Whatever."

It's annoying that she wouldn't acknowledge exactly what she'd done, but I knew it was her way of apologizing for the way she's been acting. I linked my arm through Brynn's like we used to do when we were little. "You'll always be my best friend."

She leaned into me as we walked, like she needed to be close to me. "It has been kind of weird since Sophie moved here. It changed things, you know?"

"I get it," I said. "But it's really important to me that the two of you get along. I hope you'll try to get to know Sophie a little better. If you do, I really think you'll like her."

Brynn listened without interrupting. When I finished, I felt drained and kind of nervous for what Brynn's response would be. I wasn't sure if she was going to say that it bothers her that I spend time with Sophie and that I haven't been a good friend to her since she moved here, or that she thinks Sophie likes Billy, or both, or something altogether different.

But she didn't say any of those things.

"You're right," she said. "I'd like to get to know Sophie better. Why don't you both come over tomorrow and we can all hang out."

I couldn't believe it. Sometimes I think I know Brynn so well, and then she manages to completely surprise me. "Tomorrow sounds great," I said.

"Cool!" said Brynn. "Could you check with Sophie? I don't have her number."

"Sure," I said and gave myself a virtual pat on the back.

Job well done.

Saturday, September 20, 4:59 p.m.
Home from Brynn's

Some days just don't go the way you anticipated. Sophie and I went over to Brynn's today, like we'd planned. When we first got there, it was fine. Fun actually. Brynn's mom was super sweet. "Welcome, girls!" She gave me a big hug and told Sophie she was so happy to have her over. Then she helped us make an incredible picnic lunch of hummus, pita, falafel, a salad with feta cheese and chicken in it, and baklava for dessert.

"I love Middle Eastern food," said Sophie.

"I thought you might," said Brynn's mom. She told Sophie that she had a hunch she might be an adventurous eater since Sophie has lived in so many exciting places. She asked Sophie all about living in Paris and New York. I could tell she was trying hard to make her feel comfortable, and Brynn seemed like she was too.

When we took our lunch outside, Brynn went back in and got a big blanket that she spread out on the ground. As we sat down, Brynn was telling Sophie how much she liked her jeans and sweater, and they started talking about fashion, a topic they both like.

When the conversation shifted to school, Brynn asked Sophie how she likes her classes and how they compare to her classes in New York and Paris. I was happy to see that Brynn seemed genuinely interested in Sophie.

As they talked back and forth, I started to relax. Brynn's dog, Riley, came outside and sat beside me while we ate. I fed him a piece of chicken from my salad. It was a beautiful, sunny day, and I realized how silly it had been of me to be so worried that we couldn't all be friends.

Then, as we were munching on baklava, Brynn changed the subject. "Did you have a boyfriend in New York?" she asked Sophie.

"No," said Sophie.

"Really?" Brynn said, like she was surprised.

Sophie shrugged. "No big deal."

Brynn made a *hmmm* sound, which I knew meant she thought it was a bigger deal than Sophie was letting on. "So you've never had a boyfriend? You know, like, even if it wasn't official."

Sophie didn't respond right away. I could tell she didn't like the direction the conversation had taken. I thought it was a good time to change the subject. "C'mon," I said to Brynn. "Let's jump on the trampoline. We can teach Sophie how to do a flip."

"That sounds like fun," said Sophie.

I stood up, but Brynn didn't move. "You must want a boyfriend," she said to Sophie.

"Not really," Sophie said.

"Oh, sorry," said Brynn. "I guess I just assume everyone wants a boyfriend because I have such an amazing one." Then she paused and looked directly at Sophie like she wanted her to hear every word she was about to say. "Billy and I are so close," she said. "We love hanging out. It's so cool because every time we're together, we just get closer." She smiled, like just thinking about Billy made her happy. "I wouldn't tell everyone that," she said to Sophie.

But I knew Brynn wasn't actually confiding in her. She wasn't trusting Sophie—she was sending her a message that Billy belongs to her. I looked at Sophie, but it was hard to tell what she was thinking.

I had to step in. "All this boy talk is getting boring." I grabbed Sophie and Brynn by the arms and led them over to the trampoline.

We all got on and started bouncing around. As Brynn and I demonstrated the flips we'd perfected during years of jumping, Brynn dropped the subject. I'm still not sure Sophie was aware of what Brynn was doing. Even though she's super cool in lots of ways, sometimes she seems kind of clueless when it comes to other people.

I hope she didn't know what Brynn was doing. But I knew.

And I didn't like it.

I am the poet of the Body

and I am the poet of the Soul.

—*Walt Whitman, "Song of Myself"*

Saturday, September 27, 1:15 p.m.
Busy week, no time to write

We had our first dance competition this morning, and our team did really well! Everyone was laughing and talking on the bus ride home. Brynn sat next to me, and we chatted the whole way about the other teams and how they performed. We were just a few minutes from school when I got a text from Sophie asking me if I wanted to hang out this afternoon.

Brynn looked over my shoulder at my phone and read the text. "I was going to ask you if you wanted to do something," she said.

I couldn't believe she'd read my text, and it made me kind of mad because we'd been on the bus for almost an hour and she hadn't said a word about doing anything until she read the text from Sophie. I felt like she was trying to make me choose between her and Sophie, and I wasn't going to do that.

I couldn't hang out with either of them anyway. Mom had already asked me if I'd come downtown when I got home and help her paint the store. When she'd asked me, I'd grumbled something about child labor laws and how they were enacted for a reason. I'd already babysat three nights during the week while mom sewed. But I knew Mom needed my help, so I begrudgingly agreed to do it.

I'm glad I did. I'd much rather paint than deal with this drama.

7:52 p.m.

While painting a store wouldn't be on my top ten list of fun things to do on a Saturday afternoon, I actually enjoyed it today.

Mom and I painted the walls white and one wall robin's egg blue. "It's very tranquil," said Mom. "I'm thinking about making it my signature color." She showed me samples of the other shades of blue she'd considered, and we both agreed this one was the nicest. Then she showed me where her antique sewing table was going to go and the cabinet she'd custom ordered to hold all of her fabrics. It was nice bonding time with Mom. But that wasn't what made the day so good.

When Mom and I had been painting for hours and we were both hungry, I went to the deli next door to get us some sandwiches. I had on overalls with a tank top and my hair was piled on top of my head in a messy ponytail. It was still dirty from sweating at the dance competition this morning. I wasn't thinking about what I looked like, but I wish I had been.

"What can I get you?" the guy behind the counter asked when I walked in.

I looked at him. He was skinny and tall, and he had big blue eyes and he was wearing glasses that made him look like a teacher. I read his nametag: Leo. It suited him.

I looked up at the handwritten menu behind the counter. There were way too many choices to make this easy. Leo must have been a mind reader. "First time?" he asked.

I nodded. "My mom is opening the store next door."

"Welcome to the neighborhood." He gestured to the menu behind him. "This can be overwhelming, but don't worry. It's my job to make sure you get the perfect sandwich. You can go the ham and cheese route, which I believe is greatly enhanced with honey mustard. Or you can try my favorite, which is turkey, avocado, and organic sprouts with cranberry mayo. And if neither of those appeal, knock yourself out choosing from the thirty-three options on the board behind me, or you can make something up. Dealer's choice."

I laughed. He was cute, in a funny sort of way.

"You take your sandwiches very seriously," I said.

"That I do." I looked down at the gloved hand Leo had extended in my direction. "Oops!" he said, recognizing what he'd done. He peeled off the glove and started over. "Leo," he said less formally.

"April," I said as I shook his hand. I was surprised at how warm and smooth it was, for a guy.

He read my mind again. "I have very soft hands," he said. "I always have. Or at least that's what my mother tells me." The thought of his mother telling him that made me laugh. Leo smiled. "You didn't come here for a comedy show," he said winking at me. "What will it be?"

"I'll have the turkey and avocado with sprouts and ham and cheese for my mom."

"Excellent choices, April. Might I suggest that you have both on the multigrain bread. I believe the subtle nuttiness of the crust enhances the flavor of any sandwich." It was a weird thing to say, but it sounded cute when he said it.

"Sure," I said. I bit my lip to keep from smiling. Leo looked at me and our eyes met. It was kind of embarrassing, like we both knew it had happened but there was nothing we could do about it, so we both looked away.

Leo started making the sandwiches, and I pretended to read through the choices on the menu board behind him. When he finished, he wrapped the sandwiches in butcher paper and put them in a take-out bag. "Drink and chips to go with this?" he asked.

I nodded and asked a question of my own. "What's the name of the sandwich you made for me? I don't see it anywhere on the menu board."

Leo smiled. "It's the Leo Special. I only make it for special customers."

"Am I a special customer?" I couldn't believe I'd been so flirtatious.

But Leo didn't seem to mind. "Quite possibly," he said.

I have to admit I liked his answer almost as much as his sandwich.

When in doubt, tell the truth.

—*Mark Twain*

Wednesday, October 1, 10:00 p.m.
Working on *To Kill a Mockingbird* paper
Sort of

Is it normal to be fourteen and loathe (vocab word: check!) your life?

I don't loathe my whole life, just the part of it I spend at home. If someone were to psychoanalyze me, I'm sure they'd blame me. They'd say I'm a teenager with a bad attitude. But I don't think I'm at fault here. I'm not the one who created the loathsome conditions that exist.

The problem is that Mom's store is opening

in three weeks, and it's affecting my life in many unpleasant ways.

For starters, Mom literally spends all of her time sewing, which means I'm spending all of my time babysitting when I'm not at school or dance. I think I've been a pretty good sport about it, even when I've had to do things I don't think should be my responsibility. I'm pretty sure it's the parents' job to help their young children study for a spelling test or wash a dirty soccer uniform when there are games two days in a row, right?

I can handle the babysitting and even the laundry, but what I can't handle is the arguing. And there has been lots of it lately. Not in plain view for all to see, but behind closed doors for me to hear. I know Mom and Dad are arguing in the privacy of their own room, and I shouldn't be listening in. But in my opinion, it's like playing music at full volume. Other people can't help but hear it and complain that the sound is up too high (or not say a word and just be pissed off about it). And the worst part is that they always fight about the same thing—money.

It costs a lot of money to open a store. I know this for a fact because Dad talks about it constantly. I also know that some costs are fixed and some are flexible. Writing that makes me sound like some kind of finance geek, but I'm not. I've just been spending the last several nights listening to my parents argue over which flexible costs—like having real models to model the clothes at the opening versus people we know—are necessary.

Listening to them fight about stupid stuff (and I classify this as stupid because Dad should know that no one we personally know in Faraway could even remotely fall into the model category) stresses me out.

But last night, Mom and Dad had their biggest fight ever, and it seriously upset me. It started small. They were disagreeing about the model thing, then one thing led to another. "Flora, you're being incredibly selfish and putting stress on everyone in this family," said Dad.

Mom sighed loudly enough for me to hear it through the door. "It's really disappointing how limiting your outlook on life can be," she said to Dad.

Their room got quiet after that. I held my breath and waited. Whenever they fight, they do this little thing where they say *"I love you, but I don't like you right now."* I waited outside their door for a long time, but they never said it.

So this morning, I asked Dad if he could drive me to school and on the way, I asked him if he and Mom are having problems. I thought for sure he'd say they weren't, but what he said was, "April, I prefer honesty, and yes, your mother and I are going through a difficult period."

Listening to him say that (and thinking about it all day) was highly unpleasant.

There. I think I very accurately depicted the unpleasantness at hand. It's a shame I can't turn in what I just wrote for my English paper.

Friday, October 3, 6:17 p.m.
Home from dance

Today at dance practice, we worked on the dances we're doing for the Homecoming assembly next Friday and for the half-time presentation during the game that night. The steps in both dances are really fast and working on them today took all my energy. When we finished practice, I was so tired. All I wanted to do was go home and crash on the couch.

"Wait up," said Brynn as I was leaving the gym. "I'll walk with you."

I could tell by the way Brynn rushed to catch up with me that there was something she wanted to talk to me about. She didn't waste any time telling me what was on her mind. "Do you think it's weird how Sophie and Billy are spending so much time together on SGA?"

I really didn't want to get into it with her.

I took a deep breath. "Next week is Spirit Week and Homecoming. Everyone on SGA has been working on it." Brynn knows Homecoming is one of the most important events of the school year.

"I know what week it is," said Brynn, like my explanation had been insulting and unhelpful. "I get that everyone on SGA is working on it. It's just that Sophie and Billy seem to be working very closely together." She eyed me as she talked. "Did you know they're doing a skit together to kick off Spirit Week?"

I actually didn't know that, and I was glad I could tell Brynn I didn't. It made it seem like less of a big deal.

Then I reminded Brynn that just this week, Ms. Baumann had explained that each grade would be doing group dances in the show in November. "Kids who are on SGA doing stuff together is the same thing as girls on the dance team doing dances together." I thought that was a pretty good analogy. But apparently Brynn didn't.

"Obviously," she said. Then she looked at me like she was disappointed in what I guess she perceived as my lack of depth. "Sometimes you just don't get it. Sorry if that hurts your feelings, but it's the truth." She raised a brow at me like it was my turn to apologize.

But I didn't. This wasn't about me not getting it.

It was about her being ridiculously jealous.

Saturday, October 4, 8:45 p.m.
My un-date

I had my first un-date today.

When I woke up, I had no idea that's how I'd be spending my afternoon. This morning Mom and Dad both left early, so I made breakfast for May and June. (That sounds like I made something fancy like crepes, but all I did was pour milk and cereal into bowls and slice bananas on top of it.) We ate our cereal on the couch and watched *The Sound of Music*.

It was a fun way to spend the morning. *The Sound of Music* is one of my favorite movies. I think what I like about it is that every time I watch it, I find something new that sticks out to me. This morning, I actually didn't know what that thing was, but I figured it out this afternoon. What stuck out today was the scene when the nuns tell Maria that when God closes a door, he opens a window. I needed a window to open.

I've been so stressed lately with everything going on at home. Mom opening the store has definitely made Dad feel a lot more pressure. I feel it too. Even though it has put a strain on things in lots of ways lately, today something good came out of it.

After lunch, Dad came home from the diner to take June to a birthday party. May ended up riding with them, so I walked downtown to Mom's store to help her get ready for the opening.

She was hanging black and white photos she'd taken of the clothes she designed. "These look great," I told Mom as I helped her hang them. The photos were very artsy, and I could see how ladies would like her clothes. I have to admit her store was shaping up in a cool way.

When we were done hanging photos, Mom told me I could go. "I need to do some paperwork and there's not much left here that you can help me with today." She hugged me. "Thanks so much for your help, honey."

It was midafternoon, and I was feeling good that I'd been helpful to Mom. As I left her store, I was trying to decide what I was going to do for the rest of the day, when I saw Leo. He was leaving the deli.

"April!" He sounded happy to see me.

I stopped and waited for him to catch up to me.

"What's a girl like you doing in a place like this?" he said gesturing to the mostly empty streets of downtown Faraway.

I laughed. It sounded like a line from an old movie. "I was helping my mom."

"Do I detect the use of the past tense?" asked Leo.

I nodded.

"This must be fate" said Leo. "I just finished too. If you have nothing to do, perhaps we could do it together?" He looked hopeful as he awaited my response.

"Sure," I said.

He fell in step beside me as we walked.

"Is this a date?" I asked.

Leo laughed. "Since we're doing nothing, it's more like an un-date."

"I've never been on an un-date," I told Leo.

He smiled down at me. "It's my first too. Perhaps we should start our un-date by getting to know each other. Ladies first."

As we meandered the streets of Faraway, I told Leo about my family and friends and being on the dance team. He was incredibly easy to talk to and asked lots of questions, which made me talk more. We stopped walking and sat down on a bench. I couldn't help noticing how much longer his legs were than mine. I rambled on about my life like we were old friends who hadn't seen each other in a long time and were catching up.

"Fascinating," he said when I was done.

"Not really." I couldn't image what he'd found so interesting about my life.

"I get to be the judge of that," said Leo. He smiled down at me.

"What about you?" I asked.

"I'm afraid I've led a pretty dull existence," said Leo.

"Don't I get to be the judge of that?" I asked.

"Touché," said Leo. Then he proceeded to tell me about himself. Sixteen. Only child. Homeschooled. Starting college in January.

"Wait a minute. You're only sixteen and you're going to college?"

"Guilty," said Leo.

"You must be a genius," I said.

Leo shook his head. "*Genius* is a broad term. Extreme chemistry enthusiast would probably be more accurate."

I eyed Leo carefully. "Are you homeschooled because you know more about chemistry than they teach at the high school?"

"That's part of it," said Leo.

"What's the other part?" I asked.

Leo hesitated. "I'm not sure we should get into it on our first un-date."

"Then we'll have to have a second," I said without missing a beat.

Leo smiled. "Are you flirting with me, April?"

I bit my lip. "I think so," I said quietly.

"Fascinating," said Leo.

"You like that word, don't you?"

Leo blinked at me like he was considering my question. "To be honest April, I rarely ever use it."

He that is jealous is not in love.

—*St. Augustine*

This morning there was a special assembly at school to kick off Spirit Week. Principal Meeks made a speech about Homecoming this weekend and the importance of Spirit Week. "Participate fully and show your school spirit," he said. Then he turned it over to Jeff Ingraham, a senior who's president of the SGA.

"It's going to be a great week at Faraway High!" he said. Then he went through the

Spirit Week schedule. Pajama Day Tuesday, Crazy Hat Wednesday, Red-and-White Thursday. On Friday we have the pep rally, the football game Friday night, then the dance on Saturday night.

I was sitting with Emily, Kate, and Brynn for the assembly.

"This is going to be an amazing week," said Emily.

"I already have my pajamas picked out," said Kate.

"It's going to be totally fun," I said.

We all looked at Brynn. "Yeah," she said. "It'll be great." But I could tell by her body language that she didn't really think it would be.

Before Jeff left the stage, he announced that the SGA class reps had a special presentation. Brynn sat up straight as they came out on stage in costume. The ninth-grade reps, which meant Billy and Sophie, had on pajamas. The tenth-grade reps were wearing crazy hats and the juniors were in red and white.

The skit was kind of silly. They all played dumb, like they thought today was the day they were supposed to wear pajamas or crazy hats or school colors. Then they reminded everyone to be sure and come dressed to show their spirit on the right days. When Sophie and Billy did their part about Pajama Day, I glanced at Brynn.

I could tell that watching Sophie and Billy doing the skit together was really bugging her. Their part only lasted like a minute. Still, Brynn looked upset. "You OK?" I asked.

Brynn turned and rolled her eyes at me like it was a ridiculous question. "Of course," she said. "Why wouldn't I be?"

"Sorry," I said. I figured maybe I'd read her emotions wrong. Brynn let out a breath like dealing with me was getting increasingly difficult. I guess it's not uncommon for best friends to think alike, because I was feeling the same way about her.

Wednesday, October 8
Study Hall

Sophie asked me this morning if I want to have a sleepover after the dance on Saturday.

"Sure," I said. I had no reason not to say yes. It wasn't like I had other plans.

"Great!" said Sophie. "It'll be fun!"

I agreed. But I was having a hard time thinking about the fun Sophie and I would have, because I was thinking about Brynn. I know she's upset about Sophie and Billy, but there's also still this tension between us over my friendship with Sophie. I kind of get it. If Brynn had an almost-cousin that moved to Faraway and they got super close, it would probably be hard for me too. But still, she hasn't been nice to Sophie, and I'd like to think I wouldn't act the way she has.

I've tried talking to Brynn about it, but it hasn't helped. I could invite her to our sleepover, but (a) she wouldn't want to have a sleepover with Sophie, and (b) if I did ask, she'd probably say she was going to ask me if I wanted to have a sleepover and that she can't believe I made plans with someone else.

Bottom line: I shouldn't have to choose between my two friends.

So much happened this weekend. The dance team performed at the pep rally on Friday. According to Ms. Baumann (and the applause we got), we did a great job. The Friday night football game (which we won, YEAH!) was great too. The dance team performed at halftime. It was fun and exciting and a lot less nerve racking than it was when I did it last year. When we came off the field, everyone on the team was in a great mood, including Brynn. "That was awesome!" she said and gave me a hug.

Unfortunately, the Homecoming dance on Saturday was such a weird, awkward night.

SGA had decorated the gym for the Winter Wonderland theme, and there were stars and twinkly lights everywhere. When I got to the gym, I looked around to find my friends. Sophie and Billy were in a corner hanging a string of lights. They'd been decorating all afternoon, and I guess they weren't quite done. I went over to where they were working.

"Everything looks amazing!" I told them.

"Does it look wintery?" asked Billy.

"And wonderlandy?" added Sophie.

"It's very wintery and wonderlandy," I said. Everyone was in a good mood. The three of us were talking and joking around when Brynn got to the gym. I waved to get her attention, but she wasn't looking at me. Her eyes were locked on Billy.

"You look great," I said as she joined our group. She was wearing a tight white dress that showed off all her curves.

"Thanks," she said.

"Wow!" said Billy. "You look amazing."

"I love your dress," said Sophie.

Brynn smiled and put her hand on Billy's arm. "Let's dance," she said. Then she pulled him off toward the dance floor without even acknowledging Sophie's compliment.

"She doesn't like me," Sophie said. I hadn't been sure before if Sophie was totally aware of Brynn's disdain for her, but she clearly hadn't missed it.

"She's just jealous," I said.

Sophie shrugged. "She's difficult."

Sophie is always so positive. Sometimes annoyingly so. This was the first time I'd heard her say anything so negative about someone else, and she was saying it about the person I'd been best friends with since kindergarten. "We can talk about it later," I said, not really wanting to get into it at the dance.

But Sophie didn't bring it up at our sleepover and I didn't either. I was actually relieved this morning when she left. I feel terrible saying that. Sophie hadn't done anything to me. Not directly, anyway. But she and Brynn have both made it clear they don't like each other, which puts me in the middle. The person I've always talked to when I have issues like this is Billy.

But he's clearly not a person I can talk to about this.

3:15 p.m.

I don't need to talk to Billy. The people I need to talk to are Sophie and Brynn. I just need to figure out what I want to say. They're two of my best friends and they can't not like each other. It's ridiculous. We're in high school now.

It's time they start acting like it.

I don't like that man.

I must get to know him better.

—Abraham Lincoln

Talked to Sophie

Tonight, when I got home from dance, I called Sophie and told her there's something I wanted to talk to her about.

"I'm glad you called," she said. "There's something I want to talk to you about too.

"You first," I said. I thought maybe we were going to talk about the same thing, but I wasn't expecting to hear what Sophie said.

"I was supposed to go to New York for Thanksgiving to see my dad," said Sophie. "But he called today and told me he's not coming in until Christmas."

Sophie almost never talks about her parents' situation, and when she does she makes it seem like it's no big deal, so I was a little unsure of how to respond. "That's too bad," I said.

"Yeah," said Sophie. I waited for her to elaborate, but she didn't.

"You're upset, aren't you?"

"Kind of," said Sophie. "I haven't seen my dad since we moved here." She paused. "I'm going to call him back. I know I can get him to change his mind."

"That sounds like a good idea." I've only met Sophie's dad once when he was here for Gaga and Willy's wedding. I had no idea if Sophie could get him to change his mind, but it couldn't hurt to try.

"So what did you want to talk to me about?" asked Sophie.

I hesitated. What I was going to say seemed trivial in comparison to what she'd said.

"Just say it," said Sophie, like she understood my hesitation.

I cleared my throat. "I wanted to talk to you about Brynn. She and I have been best friends since kindergarten. I know she can be . . ." I paused. I decided to use Sophie's word. "I know she can be difficult. She's just jealous of you. I really hope we can all be friends."

"Consider it done," said Sophie.

I hate to be the pessimist here, but I consider it half-done.

Friday, October 17, 6:57 p.m.
Talked to Brynn
Finally

I'd been putting off talking to Brynn all week, because sometimes she can be so unreasonable and hard to talk to. But today when I got home from dance practice, I decided to just do it. I put Gilligan on a leash and walked to her house. "Can we talk?" I asked when she came to the door.

"We're eating dinner soon," she said, like I only had a few minutes to state my case.

I got right to the point. "I want to talk to you about Sophie." Brynn stiffened. A knot started to form in my stomach. "She's part of my family," I said. "You've been my best friend since kindergarten. You're both super important to me. You can't not like each other."

"I haven't done anything," said Brynn, like Sophie was the one responsible for any tension that existed between them. I was speechless. Did Brynn actually think that was true?

"I don't have a problem with Sophie as long as she stays away from Billy," said Brynn.

It was an absurd thing to say. "She doesn't like Billy. But they're on SGA together, so that means they're going to do stuff together."

Brynn made an *hmmm* sound like she had offered to do more than her part and the rest was up to Sophie. "I have to go eat."

"That's kind of ridiculous," I said.

Brynn looked dumbfounded. "That I have to go eat?"

I let out a breath as Brynn closed the door. She knew exactly what I meant.

8:15 p.m.

I called Billy. He's Brynn's boyfriend, but he's

been one of my best friends since third grade. Plus, he knows Brynn and I have had our troubles lately, and the truth is that he's part of the problem, at least from Brynn's perspective. He listened patiently while I told him what was going on.

"I guess I don't really understand what everyone is upset about, but . . . I'm sorry you're all having issues," he said.

It was a really diplomatic response, but it didn't solve the problem. "So what do you think I should do?" I asked Billy.

"I'm honestly not sure," he said.

Billy gets an A for honesty. An F for helpfulness.

Sunday, October 19, 5:31 p.m.
Babysitting

Mom's store opens a week from yesterday, and she and Dad are both busy and stressed. This morning, she thought he was making breakfast and he thought she was making breakfast. In the time they spent discussing it, they both could have made breakfast. And lunch.

"I'll make it," I said.

I thought for sure one of them would say they were sorry for being ridiculous and that they'd be happy to do it. But they just thanked me for taking care of my sisters and left. I wasn't thrilled I had to babysit all day, but to be honest, it's better than having them around.

Wednesday, October 22
Study Hall

This morning I was trying to open my locker, but my lock was stuck. I kept turning the dial to put in my combination. But no matter what I did, it wouldn't open.

"Need some help with that?" a voice asked from behind me.

Without turning around, I knew it was Matt. I turned the dial on my lock again and pulled extra hard. Fortunately, it opened. "No, thanks," I said. Then I got out the books I needed, closed my locker, and walked off.

It was the first time we've spoken at school. Not that we spoke about much. I'd been so worried that it would be a big deal seeing him at school.

It wasn't.

Saturday, October 25
Grand opening of Flora's Fashions

Today was the opening of Mom's store. It was incredible in lots of ways, but a few things stood out that made the day especially awesome, at least for me.

The main thing was the opening itself. The store looked amazing, and so did the clothes. Everything Mom designed was black, white, coral, and robin's egg blue. All the racks of dresses, pants, skirts, and blouses were color-coordinated and so pretty. I wasn't the only one who thought so. Everybody was raving about the designs. Plus, Mom had gone all out for the opening. There were flowers, candles, food, champagne, and a harpist. Everyone was talking and toasting Mom. There was even a photographer and a reporter from the *Faraway News* who interviewed her. All of Mom's hard work showed, and I was really proud of her.

Another great thing about the night was that all my friends and family were there and everyone got along. Brynn came with her parents. Brynn's mom, who is super chic, even made an appointment to come back. "You're my new favorite designer," she said as she gave Mom a hug.

Billy was there with his family, and Sophie and her Mom came too. I was worried there would be tension between Brynn and Sophie, especially since Billy was there. But if there was, they didn't let it show. We all talked and ate finger sandwiches and laughed. It was really fun. Somehow I think they all intuitively knew how important this night was for me.

After most of the guests left, my extended family stayed. Sophie and I were hanging out with Harry, who invited us to come with him to a Halloween party that one of the juniors is having. Sophie said she'd love to go. I knew I'd have to get permission from Mom and Dad. I didn't think the opening was the time to do it, but I was excited Harry invited us. It'll be my first high school party, and I think Mom and

Dad will say yes since I'll be going with Harry and Sophie.

Another cool thing actually happened before the opening. I popped into the deli to see Leo. "Wow!" he said when he saw me. "Look at you!"

It was the reaction I'd been hoping for. I had on a fitted black dress and a pair of Mom's heels I'd had to beg her to let me wear. I was almost as tall as Leo with them on. I told Leo about the opening and that I couldn't stay long.

"That's too bad," said Leo. "I'm about to go on break."

When he said that, I took a pen off the counter and wrote my number down on a napkin and gave it to him. It felt like a very grown up thing to do.

"You can call or text me later if you want," I said.

Leo shook his head. "A call, maybe. A text, never."

"Who doesn't text?" I asked.

Leo raised his hand like he was the guilty party. "Audio is widely considered to be a core feature of phone technology. Why not use it?"

As I left, I rolled my eyes at him. But I couldn't help smiling. He's weird, but in such a likeable way.

Last but not least. When my family got home from the opening, we were all in the kitchen when Mom made a little speech. "I want to thank all of you for your support over the last month. I know it has been hard on everyone, but now that the store is up and running, things should be much smoother at home." When Mom finished talking, Dad gave her a hug. It was the first time I'd seen them be affectionate in a while, and a sense of relief washed over me. They both seemed more relaxed and happy than they'd been in a long time.

A lot of things happened today, but nothing better than this.

Charlie Brown is such a loser.

He wasn't even the star of his

own Halloween special.

—*Chris Rock*

Monday, October 27, 11:12 p.m.
Can't sleep

Just when I thought things were going to get better at home, Mom and Dad were arguing again. The good news is a woman who owns a major clothing store in Atlanta read the article about Mom that ran in the *Faraway News*. She set up a meeting with Mom at the end of November to see her clothes and said if she likes them, she might carry her line in her store.

The bad news (at least from Dad's perspective) is that Mom wants to sew a new collection made from high-end fabrics, which means she'll be spending (a) a lot of time sewing and (b) a lot of money on more fabric.

"We just spent a fortune getting the store opened. We can't afford to spend more," said Dad.

"We can't afford not to," said Mom. They went around and around on that point for a long time. Then Mom told Dad she was doing it. "The next few weeks are going to be very busy," she told him.

I didn't wait to hear Dad's response. I already know how this is going down.

Tuesday, October 28, 8:52 a.m.
School nurse's office

I forgot to set my alarm last night so I woke up late this morning. Then, when I was getting dressed, I remembered that today is the last day to bring in a check to Ms. Baumann for the dance costumes for the show. She'd gone on record saying that if you don't have a check by practice today, you can't dance in the show. So I threw on clothes, skipped makeup entirely, and was in the kitchen trying to quickly explain to Mom why I needed a check for $122.19 on the spot when June walked in in her pajamas.

"Why aren't you dressed?" asked Mom.

"I'm not going to school," said June as she sat down at the table.

"Do you feel sick?" Mom went over to June and put a hand on her forehead. "You don't have a fever." June crossed her arms across her chest.

I cleared my throat. "Um, Mom, I need a check now or I'm going to be late."

Mom gave me a blank look like she'd forgotten what we'd been discussing. She turned her attention back to my sister. "You have to go to school."

June shook her head. "I'm not going. Cole Martin is mean to me. And so are Sam Chen and Evan Walker."

I blew out a breath. "Mom, I need a check. Now."

"How are they mean?" she asked in response.

"They make fun of me because I bring soy milk in my lunch."

"Tell them you're allergic to dairy," said Mom.

June shook her head like that wouldn't work. "They'll say I'm weird. That's what they say every day." Mom sat down at the table and took a sip of coffee, like that was going to give her some insight as to how to handle the situation.

I looked at the clock. I was seriously going to be late for homeroom. "Tell them they're all big baby losers and you'll beat them up if they make fun of you again," I said.

"April!" Mom said my name sharply.

"Mom!" I said shoving her checkbook in front of her. "I'm really late." So she wrote the check, but not until she told me I need to be more responsible and let her know in advance when I need money for something. It stressed me out and made me wonder if she didn't want to write the check because we don't have the money, but it also made me have to run to school. I literally ran all the way. When I got to

Mrs. Monteleone's room, she was just finishing taking the role. Beads of sweat were running down my forehead.

"I'm going to have to give you an unexcused tardy," she said as I entered her classroom. I'm not sure what the consequences of having an unexcused tardy are, but shockingly, Mrs. Monteleone changed her mind. She said she wasn't giving me the tardy because I looked feverish, then she sent me to the nurse's office.

The nurse took my temperature, then gave me some juice and a paper towel and told me I could sit out first period while I cool down.

The only problem is I sweated so much, now I have body odor.

I'd much rather have the unexcused tardy.

Wednesday, October 29, 7:32 p.m.
In my room

Mom asked me if I could stop by the store after dance practice and help her set up a Flora's Fashions Facebook page. I thought she could have figured it out without me, but

I didn't think it was a good time to say no. When I'd asked if I could go to Mark Miller's Halloween party with Harry and Sophie, she and Dad had reluctantly agreed. I didn't want her to change her mind.

Once we had her Facebook page set up, she had some paperwork to do before we left, so I went next door to see if Leo was there. He was busy slicing meat, but he took a break. "I'm glad you came," he said. "I was going to call you tonight."

"You really don't text, do you?"

Leo shook his head. "If you have something to say, just say it."

I couldn't help but smile. "So why were you going to call me?" I asked.

"I wondered if you would like to go trick-or-treating with me on Halloween."

I sighed. The idea of trick-or-treating with him was appealing, but I'd already made plans. "I can't," I said.

Leo shook his head like not going was a mistake. "Trick-or-treating will be retro and fun. We'll get to eat loads of candy."

"It sounds like fun, but I already told my cousins Harry and Sophie that I'd go with them to a party." I shrugged. "I mean, I think the party will be fun."

"April, high school parties are not fun for 98 percent of the kids who attend them."

I laughed. "Is that a fact?"

Leo shook his head. "Nope. Just a theory."

Thursday, October 30, 6:46 p.m.
Home from dance

As we were leaving dance, Brynn asked what I'm doing for Halloween, so I told her I'm going to Mark Miller's party. She wrinkled her nose when I said it. "Who are you going with?"

Everyone knew about his party and that mostly upperclassmen were invited. I'm sure she was wondering how I got invited. "Harry," I said. "And Sophie." I debated telling Brynn that part. There hadn't been any issues with her and Sophie since I'd talked to Brynn about it, and I'd like to keep it that way. But still, I didn't want to lie about who I was going with.

Brynn winced. "Do you think it'll be fun,

you know, since there won't be many freshmen there?" She shrugged. "I don't know. If it were me, it seems like it would be weird."

I couldn't tell if she was genuinely concerned, or upset that she wasn't invited, or jealous I was going to be with Sophie on Halloween. I wanted to change the subject. "What are you doing?" I asked.

She smiled. "Billy and I are *staying in*." She emphasized the words as she said them, then looked at me. "Know what I mean?"

"Yeah," I said, though I wasn't completely sure I did. I didn't like thinking about what it meant that Brynn and Billy were *staying in* together on Halloween.

I'm also not sure I liked her response about the party. At first, it didn't really bother me, but I thought about it all the way home. It feels like, by saying I wouldn't have fun, she was putting some kind of Halloween hex on me.

Well, everyone knows there's no such thing as hexes.

Are there?

Just when we think we've figured things out, the universe throws us a curveball.

—*Meredith Grey*, Grey's Anatomy

Halloween, 6:45 p.m.
Getting ready

I can't decide if I should wear ripped blue jeans with a black top, black jeans with a black top, or black jeans with an orange top. I just asked May (because she happened to come into my room while I was trying to decide), who said I should wear the ripped blue jeans with an orange top, which technically wasn't one of the choices, but part of me thinks she might be right (even though she's never right

101

when it comes to clothes). Since Mom is a fashion designer I'm going to the kitchen to ask her what she thinks I should wear.

7:17 p.m.
Back from the kitchen

I'm back from the kitchen, and there was no point in going. When I asked Mom what she thought I should wear to the party, she pursed her lips like she was actually considering my question (which it turns out wasn't the case). Before she could answer, June put in her two cents. "I think you should wear a pirate costume or go as a ghost."

Mom unpursed her lips. "April, do you really think it's a good idea to go to this party?"

I'd already been over this with Mom and Dad, and I didn't think I should have to do it again, especially when I had more important things to be doing, like getting ready. "I think it's a great idea. I'm going with Harry and Sophie. Aren't you happy I'm spending time with family?"

Mom shook her head like that wasn't the

issue. "It's just that there will be older kids there. I've heard these parties can get pretty out of control."

I let out a breath and tried to stay patient. I knew if I got frustrated Mom would take it as a sign that I wasn't "mature" enough to go. "Mom, don't worry. I'll be careful. I promise."

That seemed to get the job done because after a long lecture about the dangers of underage drinking and the importance of not succumbing to peer pressure, Mom agreed (even though she'd already agreed) that I could go, which was great, though it didn't answer the what-should-I-wear question.

The answer is I'm going with black and black. Sophie just called and said that's what she's wearing and that one thing she learned from living in New York is that you can never go wrong with all black. Then she said tonight should be really fun and that she can't wait to go.

Neither can I. Happy Halloween! I'm going to a party!!!

8:32 p.m.

Group text

Harry: Be there in 5.

Sophie: Where?

Sophie: My house?

Me: Or my house?

Sophie: ???

Me: ???

Harry: April.

Me: What?

Harry: Your house first.

Me: OK. See ya.

Sophie: Hurry!

Harry: Ur annoying.

Sophie: WHO???

Harry: Both of you.

Me: Hurry up!

Sophie: Yeah!

Harry: Chill!

Sophie: ☺

Me: 😄

Harry: It's Halloween.

Me: 🎃

Sophie: 🎃

Sophie: Stop texting and hurry up!
Harry: I'm coming.
Harry: 🎃

Saturday, November 1, 10:57 a.m.
Sophie just left
Worst Halloween ever

I can't believe I was so excited to go to
the party last night. It was literally the worst
Halloween ever (and last Halloween, when all
my friends were mad at me for kissing Matt
when Billy and I were together, was pretty
awful). I should have taken it as a sign when
Mom tried to talk me out of going to the party.
Actually, it was like a third sign. Leo had tried
to talk me out of it first. Then Brynn said it
didn't sound like fun. Then Mom. I should
have listened to one of them.

I could sugarcoat it (dumb Halloween
reference) and write about the good parts of the
night that led up to the bad part. I did have fun
walking to the party with Harry and Sophie,
ringing doorbells to get candy, then joking
around as we threw candy to each other and

tried catching it in our mouths. But what's the point when what happened when we got to the party overshadowed all that?

At first, everything was cool. Mark's backyard was packed. Some seniors, but mostly juniors and sophomores, and a few kids from my class. Sophie and Harry and I were all hanging out. After a while, Harry drifted off with some friends and kind of disappeared.

Sophie and I were talking to the kids who were there from our grade when Chase Campbell, a junior on the football team and widely considered to be the hottest guy at school, started talking to Sophie. I could tell Sophie wasn't that into him, but he was telling her some long story about something that happened at a game, and she couldn't really walk off while he was in the middle of it. I felt like a third wheel just standing there, so I walked off.

I wasn't sure what to do with myself. I didn't want it to look like I didn't have anyone to talk to so I just started walking like I had somewhere to go. I walked to the back of

Mark's yard. There were a bunch of trees and a tool shed, so I thought I could kind of hang out there undetected while Sophie talked to Chase, but that turned out to be a HUGE mistake.

Matt Parker was there, making out with Libby Walker, a cheerleader in his class. He was sitting on the ground with his back against the tool shed and Libby was sitting in his lap facing him. Her back was to me, and Matt's hands were on her butt. I couldn't see her face, or his, but I could tell by the way the way they were kissing that they were into it.

It wasn't like I wanted to be looking at them, but I couldn't help it. I just stood there staring. Then the worst thing happened. Matt and Libby stopped kissing for a second, and when they did, he looked up like he wanted to make sure no one else was back there, and he saw me standing there watching them. Our eyes locked. He stared at me for a few seconds, then he went back to kissing Libby like I wasn't even there.

I felt the party spinning around me. I went back to where Sophie was talking to Chase, and several of his teammates had joined them. My heart was racing as they talked. It's one thing to see Matt on my street while I'm walking my dog or at school while I'm trying to open my locker, but it's a whole other thing to see him at a party making out with another girl.

"What do you think?" I heard Sophie's voice. Everyone was looking at me like I was supposed to answer the question. I opened my mouth to speak, but nothing came out.

"Is she a mute for Halloween?" some guy asked. People laughed.

Sophie took my arm. "Excuse us," she said and led me to the bathroom. When we got there, I sank down onto the floor. Sophie sat down beside me and I told her about seeing Matt kissing Libby and how he saw me watching them.

"You didn't do anything wrong," said Sophie. "If people make out at a party, there's a good chance other people are going to see them."

"I know. But why did I have to stand there staring? It was so embarrassing." Sophie looked at me. I think she got that embarrassment wasn't the only issue. She leaned against me, and we sat quietly like that for a long time. Finally, Sophie broke the silence. "I called my dad. He's not coming for Thanksgiving."

"I'm sorry," I said. I put my head on her shoulder.

We didn't move until someone started banging on the door. "Want to go?" she asked.

I nodded and we left the party. As we walked home, I asked Sophie about her conversation with her dad. "I don't want to talk about it," she said. Then she changed the subject and talked about boys and how they can be jerks and that Matt is at the top of that list.

"He saw me looking at him. That's just so embarrassing."

Sophie laughed. "He's the one who should be embarrassed."

She was trying to cheer me up. In my head, I knew what she was saying was true, but I couldn't help that it hurt seeing him with another girl.

Sophie and I had already planned to have a sleepover after the party. When we got to my house, we went to my room and got in bed, but I couldn't sleep. I was tossing and turning and thinking about what I saw at the party. Then, the all-too-familiar sounds of my parents arguing drifted into my room from their room across the hall. It was bad enough listening to my parents fight, but worse that Sophie had to hear them too.

"Sorry," I said even though I hadn't done anything wrong.

"It's OK," said Sophie. "Boys suck and so do parents."

It was a such a dark, out-of-character comment from Sophie, but it had a lullaby effect on me, and I think her too, because we both closed our eyes.

I don't even remember falling asleep.

The moment you doubt

whether you can fly, you cease

forever to be able to do it.

—*Peter Pan*

Saturday, November 1, 11:47 a.m.
In my room

Harry just called. I'm not sure if it's because Sophie called him when she left and told him he should or if he just thought he should. "I saw Matt and Libby last night," he said without wasting any time on hellos. "Is that why you left?" he asked.

"Yep."

"Matt's a jerk," said Harry.

I let out a breath. "You've said that before."

"And I was right."

Harry was trying to make me feel better. I appreciated his loyalty, and he *was* right. Matt is a jerk. But he has a sweet side too. He was so cute when he asked me out that day at the beach and when he used to hang out with me and my sisters and do things like rake pine needle houses or play Monopoly.

I don't even know why I'm thinking about all that. Whether Matt is a jerk or sweet, or some of both, doesn't erase the fact that I watched him make out at a party with another girl.

That hurt.

Sunday, November 2, 6:45 p.m.
In a downward spiral

While I was walking Gilligan today, Matt came outside. He didn't have Matilda with him, so it wasn't like he went outside to walk his dog. He caught up to me like he had something he wanted to say to me. For once, he spoke first. "It was kind of creepy how you were staring at Libby and me."

I couldn't believe what he'd said or that he used the word *creepy* to describe me. *Creepy* was being confronted on my street when I was walking my dog. "I wasn't staring at you." I wanted my words to sound angry, not defensive. I'm not sure Matt picked up on it.

He shrugged. "It seemed like you were."

I couldn't believe how insensitive he was being. "I wasn't staring. I was surprised. I wasn't expecting to see you at a party making out with another girl."

Matt pursed his lips. "You know we broke up."

"I know," I said with a big nod—like, *of course* I know. Then I grabbed Gilligan by the leash, turned, and walked home.

There were a lot of things I should have said. *I'm glad. You're a jerk. Wish we'd never gone out in the first place.* But I didn't. I think I was too shocked. It was the most Matt Parker had ever had to say.

I never thought I'd say this, but I like him more when he's quiet.

8:17 p.m.

Things just keep getting worse. When I got out of the shower, Mom was in my room sitting on my bed. "April, can you come into the den, please? Dad and I would like to talk to you."

"I have a towel on." I gestured to the water still dripping down from my hair.

"Dry off and put on your pajamas," said Mom. "We'll be waiting."

When I got there, May and June were already sitting on the couch. I sat beside them and eyed my parents. Mom and Dad were both standing, and Dad had his arms crossed. They both looked tense, especially Dad. "Why are we having a family conference?" I asked.

Mom looked like she was glad someone had asked that question, though my intention hadn't been to be helpful. I mainly just wanted out of there.

"Girls, your father and I want to talk to you," said Mom. "I have an opportunity to present my line to a store in Atlanta at the end of the month. It would be a huge deal if they carry my clothes." She paused and looked at Dad. His face was expressionless.

This was old news to me.

Mom continued. "It's going to mean a lot of work for me over the next few weeks. I'm going to need all of you to pitch in and help out." Then, as she talked about how she would be working day and night to get the clothes ready in time, and that it would mean I'd be taking care of May and June while she was at the store and Dad was at the diner, my mind blanked. I don't even know what all she said.

"Got it?" I heard Mom say. She was done talking and looking at me.

"I got it," I said.

But it doesn't mean I like it.

Monday, November 3, 11:14 a.m.
Study Hall

This morning I was at my locker when I saw Matt walking down the hall toward me. He actually slowed down as he got closer to me. I'd like to believe he was going to stop and apologize for what he said last night. But I have no idea what he was going to say because I didn't give him an opportunity. Right when he passed me, I looked down like I was busy dealing with my lock and didn't see him. I should have looked up. Not so much to hear what he had to say, but to tell him what I was thinking, which is that what Harry said about him is true. But I didn't.

Guess I wasn't in the mood.

3:35 p.m.
Feeling like a loser

I told Sophie what happened this morning at my locker. "I should have said something when I had the chance."

"It's not the kind of conversation you have at your locker before school," she said.

I agreed with her, but I think the real reason I didn't talk to Matt is because I know he won't care what I have to say.

I don't like him anymore, but seeing him with someone else made me wonder what went wrong when we went out. Was he pissed I went to summer camp? Or that I didn't let him touch my boobs? Maybe that's why he was with Libby. Did she let him touch her boobs? At a party? Does it make me a loser that I wouldn't do that? I don't think it does.

So why do I feel like one?

Wednesday, November 5, 6:05 p.m.
Babysitting

Maybe the reason I feel like a loser is because I am one. When I got home from dance, Mom asked me to babysit. "You can heat up the leftover meatloaf from last night," she said.

"Can we eat in front of the TV?" asked May.

"Can we watch *SpongeBob*?" asked June.

Technically, I'm not sure what the definition of a loser is, but someone who eats leftover meatloaf on the couch with her little sisters while watching a show about a demented sponge can't be far off.

Thursday, November 6, 7:10 p.m.
Babysitting
Again

When I got home from dance, Mom asked me if I could babysit again. It was a repeat performance of last night.

Only difference: lasagna instead of
meatloaf.

Friday, November 7, 8:45 p.m.
In a rut

Tonight makes my babysitting average three
for three.

While most kids my age are at football
games or parties on a Friday night, I'm
home babysitting and eating grilled cheese
sandwiches. Which isn't the worst thing in the
world because we're having tomato soup with
the sandwiches, which is the most exciting
thing I can think to write about.

Sad. Very sad.

Saturday, November 8, 2:45 p.m.
Feeling sick

We had an extralong dance practice this
morning. We're in full practice mode since
the dance show is at the end of the month. I
was completely exhausted because I couldn't
fall asleep until after two. I could barely follow
the steps of the freshman modern dance we're

working on for the show. Ms. Baumann called me out twice and during our break. I was so relieved when practice ended. All I wanted to do was go home and take a nap.

But as I was leaving, Brynn caught up to me. "Are you OK?" she asked.

"Yeah," I said. "I'm just tired."

Brynn shook her head like she knew that wasn't it. "You can't fool me," she said. "We've been best friends for a long time. Did something happen?"

It made me feel good she knew me well enough to ask, so I told her what happened at the party and how Matt confronted me on the street. "That sucks," she said. Then she changed the subject. I'd like to believe it was because she got that I didn't want to keep talking about Matt. But I think it was because she had something she really wanted to tell me. "April, something happened. It's big." Brynn shrugged. "You should know."

I nodded like I was listening.

"Do you remember I told you that Billy was coming over on Halloween?"

"Yeah." My gut told me I wasn't going to like what was coming next.

"We were on my bed watching a movie," said Brynn slowly. "Then we started kissing." She looked at me like she wanted to gauge my reaction.

I tried to remain expressionless. Even though part of me didn't want to hear what she had to say, another part of me needed to know everything. "We kissed for a long time," said Brynn. "Then one thing led to another." She hesitated. "We took the next step."

I watched as she put her hand on her chest. She looked like she was about to say the Pledge of Allegiance. I wanted to believe that's what she Billy did together, but I knew it wasn't what she meant.

I tried to swallow but couldn't. All I could think about was how big Brynn's boobs had gotten in the last year and how the three of us had been best friends since third grade and now Brynn and Billy were close in this new way I couldn't be part of.

"So?" said Brynn when she finished talking.

I wasn't sure what my response should be. *Congrats?* "That's cool," I said.

Brynn grinned like that was the response she was hoping for. "Thanks for being happy for me." Then she looped her arm through mine as we walked like we were still in kindergarten. "It's just really cool how close Billy and I are. It makes me so happy."

"Yeah," I said. I knew she wanted me to share in her happiness, but I was having a hard time doing it. Especially since all I could think about was my own unhappiness and the slump I've been in since Halloween.

My parents are stressed and fighting and never home. All I ever do is babysit. My exboyfriend was at a party making out with another girl. Brynn and Billy are doing things together I don't like thinking about. And even though things seem OK for the moment, I know Sophie and Brynn don't really like each other.

I really don't know what I expected when I started high school.

Not this.

It is often when night looks darkest,

that one senses the gathering

momentum for change.

—*Hillary Clinton*

Monday, November 10, 6:45 p.m.
Rainy day

It poured all day, which most kids at Faraway High complained about. Some of the walkways between the buildings aren't covered so it's impossible to avoid getting wet between classes. But I didn't care. The rain was a welcome shield between the rest of the world and me. I'm just not in the mood for other people.

When I got home from dance practice, June

was in the kitchen putting miniature apple juice boxes and water bottles in the refrigerator. "April, look!" she said. "Dad went to Costco and bought these for me to take in my lunch. Now no one will make fun of me anymore."

"That's great!" I said.

June let out a big sigh of relief. "I feel so much better!"

I wish all my problems could be solved by a trip to Costco.

Tuesday, November 11, 7:12 p.m.
In the bathtub
Trying to relax

At dance practice, Ms. Baumann made her the-show-is-in-two-weeks-so-get-ready-to-work-harder-than-you-ever-have speech. I remember it from last year. Then, I thought she was just trying to scare us. Now, I know she means every word of it. The dance show is such a big deal in Faraway. It's always good and so many people go to see it.

"I'm so focused," said Emily as we walked

home from practice. "This dance show is my top priority. It's even more important to me than school right now. I just want the whole show to be amazing."

I get why she would say that. Emily is dancing the freshman solo, which is a huge honor. I know how important it is to her that her dance is the best it can be. I know I need to focus too, but that won't be easy.

Today as we practiced the intro group dance, my brain was running off in so many directions. Every time I looked at Brynn, I thought about what she told me about Billy and her. I was thinking about Sophie, who told me at lunch that as ninth-grade reps, she and Billy are co-chairs of the SGA Thanksgiving food drive. That made me think even more about Brynn and how she will react when she finds out. I was thinking about everything going on at home. And I was trying not to think about Matt, who I don't like thinking about.

As I walked with Emily, my brain drifted as she talked about the show. "Do you get what

I'm saying about the importance of focus?"
Emily asked interrupting my thoughts.

"I do," I said. "I'm focused."

Just on all the wrong things.

Thursday, November 13, 6:56 p.m.

Today at dance practice, Brynn was acting
so weird. During break, I went up to her and
asked her if she was OK. "Fine," she said
with the fake smile she only makes when
she's not fine. Then she turned away from
me and started talking to Kate and Vanessa
like I'd interrupted their conversation. She
wouldn't even look at me during the rest of
practice.

When we were done I went up to her again.
"Do you want to do our algebra homework
together?" I asked. Mr. Baumgartner had given
us a huge packet of problems, and I thought
it would be a lot easier for both of us if we
worked on them together.

Brynn looked at me like I'd asked her to slit
her wrists. "Did you know Sophie and Billy
are co-chairing the food drive?"

"Yeah," I said. I didn't like where this was going.

Brynn shook her head. "Why didn't you tell me?"

"The ninth-grade SGA reps are always head of the food drive, so of course they're doing it together."

Brynn ignored the logic of what I'd said. "I know Sophie is your sort-of cousin, but it bothers me that she keeps doing things with my boyfriend. You know as well as I do that she's never had a boyfriend. I just don't believe her when she says she doesn't want one. I think she wants mine."

I took a deep breath. "Don't you think you're being a little irrational?"

"How can you say that about me?" asked Brynn.

I had to protect Sophie. "Sophie doesn't like Billy in that way." I paused. "And I don't like when you say bad things about her." The words sat between us like an electric fence. "You know, I can be friends with both of you."

Brynn made an *hmmm* sound. "Yeah, well

friends can discuss anything, which clearly doesn't apply to us."

Then she turned and walked out of the gym. Which is a good thing, because I don't want to think about what I would have said if she'd stayed.

10:16 p.m.
Should I call Brynn?

I've been thinking a lot about what happened with Brynn this afternoon and trying to decide if I should call. When she walked out of the gym, I think she expected me to go after her and tell her I was sorry for not telling her about the food drive, or that even though Sophie is my "sort-of" cousin, what she said about her is valid and that she'll always be my best friend.

I thought about it. But Brynn hasn't exactly been a good best friend lately. And in comparison to Sophie, she hasn't been a good friend at all. Should I call her?

I'm going with no.

Billy called me. He just called to say hi and see what was going on, but it seemed kind of ironic that he called me when he did. "You're kind of quiet," he said after I'd answered a whole string of questions with *yes* or *no*. "What's up?"

He'd asked, so I decided to tell him. "Sometimes Brynn can be a lot to handle," he said when I was done. His response made me feel bold. There was something I'd wanted to ask him for a long time. If ever there was a time, this was it. But still, I knew I probably shouldn't.

"What is it?" asked Billy. He laughed and so did I. We both knew I wanted to ask him something. "I guess I'm just wondering . . ." My voice trailed off as I lost my nerve.

"What?" asked Billy.

I took a breath. "I guess I'm just wondering what it is that you like about Brynn. I mean, as a girlfriend."

Billy always thinks before he responds, but it didn't take him long to answer my question.

"Well, for one thing, she's loyal," he said. I knew what he meant, but hadn't said. He'd only had one other girlfriend. Me. And that was the one thing I hadn't been.

Ouch.

Friday, November 14, 10:45 p.m.
In my room

This is what I overheard tonight from my parents' room:

Mom: I need her to come in and help wait on customers tomorrow while I sew. The presentation is in a week and a half, and I'm not ready.

Dad: April has dance practice in the morning, and I thought she was going to babysit May and June in the afternoon.

Mom: Why don't they go with you to the diner?

Dad: I can't watch them while I work.

Mom: They're big girls. They can hang out in your office or help if you need them to.

Dad: It works better if April stays home with her sisters.

Mom: I need her help at the store.
Dad: I think it works best for everyone
if she stays home.

Usually, listening to my parents argue is
bad, but listening to them debate what I should
do was making me furious. Plus, I thought Dad
was being unfair. He could take May and June.
They're more than old enough to spend an
afternoon at the diner.

I got out of bed and marched into their
room. "You know I can hear every word you're
saying." I looked at both of them like I was
disgusted by their behavior.

"I'm in high school now. I'm old enough
to speak for myself." I turned my attention to
Mom. "I'll be there tomorrow." Then I went
back to my room.

I need some sleep.

Apparently, I have customers to wait on.

Saturday, November 15, 1:02 p.m.
Grumpy

Dance sucked. Practice was hard. Plus,
Brynn was being so annoying. Every time I

said something, she had this look on her face like it was painful for her to listen. I knew she thought I owed her an apology, but I wasn't giving her one. I've always been the one to give in to her, but she's been unfair about Sophie ever since she moved here. I had nothing to apologize for.

Then, when I came home, May and June were waiting for me. "Dad said you have to make lunch for us," said May. "Then he's going to pick us all up and drop you off at the store and we're going with him to the diner."

It pissed me off. The diner serves food, so I don't see why Dad couldn't make lunch for his daughters. But I clearly didn't get to offer an opinion on this matter.

I took out a loaf of bread and a package of ham. I lined three slices of bread up on the counter and slapped two pieces of ham on top of each one. I topped off the ham with another slice of bread. "Here," I said sliding the sandwiches across the counter to May and June.

June looked at hers. "I want turkey."

"Just eat it," I snapped.

May and June recoiled. "Why are you so grumpy?" asked May.

I took a bite of my own sandwich and ignored her question. She wouldn't understand the answer anyway.

10:45 p.m.

Less grumpy

I'm glad I went to help Mom at her store. It was a temporary respite (vocab word, well used) from my chronic bad mood. Not that waiting on ladies while they shopped for clothes was particularly inspiring, but what happened afterward was. When the store closed, I went next door to the deli.

"Want some therapy?" Leo asked when I walked in.

"Huh?" I couldn't believe it was that evident that I was having a bad day.

Leo smiled. "That's deli code for chicken soup." He motioned for me to sit down at a table. He went into the kitchen, and when he returned, he brought back a steaming bowl of chicken noodle soup that he set in front of me.

I took a spoonful. "That's hot!" I said as I downed a glass of water.

Leo laughed. "Soup usually is." Then he got a serious look on his face. "What's up April? You look troubled."

It all spilled out. Everything. I told Leo about my parents and how they're always arguing and stressed and expect me to do so much. I told him about the drama with Brynn and that she doesn't like Sophie because she thinks Sophie is trying to steal Billy, and that she's mad at me because she thinks I'm taking Sophie's side over hers. And I told him what happened on Halloween. I told him about seeing Matt and that, even though I don't like him anymore, it didn't feel good seeing him with another girl. I even told him what Matt said to me on the street and how I didn't confront him when I had the chance.

Leo listened patiently until I was done. "This is like a very complex chem lab," he said. "But the good news is that I have a solution."

"What does chem have to do with my problems?"

"That was a science joke. Chem lab. Problem. Solution. Get it?" Leo didn't wait for me to laugh. "First, parents. They can be a handful," said Leo.

He told me about his own family and that he's been listening to his parents argue since he was little. "Sometimes I think the only thing they have in common is me. The way I look at it is that parents are people too. which means they go through ups and downs. I think the best you can do is look at what really motivates them and how they feel about you."

It was reassuring to hear that. Even though things have been difficult lately, I know what my parents love most is their family and that they'd do anything for my sisters and me.

"When it comes to your crazy friends, I'm afraid I can't be of much help," said Leo.

I frowned. "My friends aren't crazy."

"In my experience, most teens are," said Leo. "That's why I'm homeschooled."

"I thought you said you had a solution."

Leo gave me a sheepish smile. "I do. The solution is simple." Then he said something I totally hadn't expected.

"Come with me to yoga."

Waking up to who you are

requires letting go of who you

imagine yourself to be.

—*Alan Watts*

Saturday, November 22, 9:45 p.m.
Post-yoga

I went to yoga with Leo tonight, and in a weirdly Zen way, I liked it.

Leo doesn't live too far from me, so he walked to my house and we walked to the yoga studio together. It was the first time I'd told Mom and Dad about him. I think normally they'd have a problem with me hanging out with a guy who's sixteen, but they've been so distracted lately with their own problems, that when I told them I was going with Leo to yoga, they didn't even question it.

When we got to the yoga studio, Leo introduced me to the teacher, Natasha, who gave me a mat and told me to go at my own pace. Leo set his mat up next to mine. "Don't do what I do," he said with a wink.

But as the class started, I couldn't believe how good he was. He moved from posture to posture in a strong yet graceful way. I was pretty self-conscious at first. But as Natasha led the class through Sun Salutation, she told us to focus on our breathing and to allow our lungs to fill with air. As I concentrated on my breathing, I stopped worrying about what other people were doing and started to relax.

As Natasha went through the rest of the poses, I followed her lead and tried my best to do what she was showing us. My favorite pose was called camel pose. It's like doing a backbend while you're on your knees and it was a great stretch.

We finished the class with something called corpse pose or Savasana. You lie flat on your back with your arms and legs spread out and your eyes closed, and you just breathe as a way of meditating. It was incredibly relaxing. I almost fell asleep while we were doing it.

I probably would have, but Natasha was going from person to person rubbing lavender oil on everyone's temples. When she got to me, I took a deep breath as she massaged the sides of my head, and my nostrils filled with the scent of lavender and burning incense.

Before we left the class, we all sat on our knees and held our hands in prayer position.

"Each day is a new opportunity. The unexpected can happen. Embrace it," said Natasha. "Move forward without expectation and with gratitude for what is, not worrying about what will be." Her voice had a soothing quality.

"Namaste," she said. Then the whole class said "Namaste." People bowed and then started picking up their mats.

"What'd you think of yoga?" asked Leo as we walked home.

"You're amazing at it."

Leo smiled. "It just takes practice. Maybe we'll do it again sometime."

"I'd like that," I said.

Leo took in my expression. "You look puzzled."

It's so cool how Leo is able to get what I'm thinking without me saying anything. "There's something I'm not sure I get," I said.

Leo raised an eyebrow.

I'd been mulling over what Natasha said at the end of the class. "What do you think Natasha meant when she talked about moving forward without expectation?"

Leo was uncharacteristically slow to answer. I'm not sure if he was relaxed from the class or formulating his response. "When I started high school, I had an expectation of what it would be like. Middle school was hard for me. I didn't fit in, and I was sure it would change when I got to high school. I thought the kids would think it was cool that I was so smart." Leo paused. "But they thought it was weird. They called me Lab Rat. Burner Boy. Broke my glasses. Kid stuff, but I didn't like it. It's why I wanted to be homeschooled."

So this was the part of his story he hadn't felt comfortable sharing with me when we first talked about why he is homeschooled. I tried to imagine what it would be like to feel so different from the other kids. I'm sure it was hard.

Leo kept talking. "Now I'm going to college, and I'm trying to have no expectations of what it will be like. I don't want to be disappointed."

"Do you think having expectations always leads to disappointment?" I asked.

"No," said Leo. "Sometimes things happen that are better than what you expected. But if you expect things to go a certain way or that people will act how you want them to, you'll just be disappointed if they don't."

He looked down at me over the rim of his glasses. "Like with Brynn. If you expect that she's going to embrace Sophie, you'll be disappointed if that's not what happens."

"I get what you're talking about," I said. "But isn't it kind of unrealistic not to have expectations?"

"I'm not saying it's not hard. But what's the point? If you don't have expectations, you avoid disappointment." I was quiet as I thought about what he'd said. Leo continued. "And with Matt. If you don't expect him to be a nice guy, you won't be disappointed when he's a jerk."

I made a face.

"Sorry if that was hard for you to hear," said Leo. "You can't control what other people do."

That made sense. "But what do I do? Just let Matt go on being a jerk?"

Leo shook his head. "Absolutely not. You tell him how you feel."

I looked down. "He doesn't care how I feel."

Leo shrugged. "It's not about him. It's about you." His eyes met mine. "I know more about chemistry in a lab than chemistry between people, but I think you need closure with Matt."

"If I have something to say, just say it."

Leo did a fist pump. "Tell him how you feel, and be done."

Leo was right, and I knew it. Matt didn't turn out to be the person I thought he was, and it's time for me to move on. Once and for all. As we walked, a comfortable silence settled between Leo and me. "You're so good at so many things," I said. "Chemistry. Yoga. Knowing what to say to make people feel better. Is there anything you don't know how to do?"

Leo laughed. "No one knows how to do everything."

I knew that was the case, but I wanted to know where Leo was deficient. "Name one thing you don't know how to do," I said.

"Are you serious?"

I stopped walking and leaned against a tree. I looked at Leo like I was waiting for him to give me an answer.

"OK," said Leo. He stopped walking too and turned to face me. "One thing I don't know how to do is kiss a girl."

I hadn't expected him to say that. "You've never kissed a girl?" I asked softly.

Leo shook his head. Even though it was dark outside, I could see that his face was turning red. I took Leo's hands in mine and put them around my waist. He looked at me and silently moved closer. I reached up and circled my arms around his neck. Leo is taller than I am, so I stood on my tiptoes. Our mouths were almost aligned.

I tilted my chin toward his, our lips met, and we kissed. It wasn't a long kiss, just a few seconds, but it felt instinctive and comfortable, like . . . like we'd kissed each other before. When we were done, I pulled back, and Leo looked at me. "What did you think of kissing?" I asked.

"I think you're amazing at it."

I smiled at Leo. "It just takes practice. Maybe we'll do it again sometime."

"I'd like that," said Leo. Then he ruffled the top of my hair with his hand. "You're cute, April."

I reached up and did the same thing to his hair. "So are you, Leo." We both laughed and as he walked me home, and I felt my lungs fill up with air.

Happy air.

I talked to Matt. I did it, and it was simple. I went to his house after lunch, rang the bell, and when he opened the door, I told him what I'd come to say. No hesitation.

"When we started going out, you were sweet. I really liked you, and I thought you liked me too. But you hurt me this summer when you kissed Sophie while I was at camp. You didn't even seem like you were sorry you did it. You said we'd see what things were like when school started. Then you kissed a girl at a party I happened to be at, and when I saw you do it, you told me I'm creepy."

Matt opened his mouth like he was going to say something, but I didn't give him an opportunity. "It doesn't matter what happened," I said. "You didn't turn out to be the person I thought you were."

"April," said Matt, and he paused. Then he did his head bob thing. I don't know if he was stalling while he was thinking of what he wanted to say or if that was all he had to say. Either way, it didn't matter. I was done. I turned and walked back to my house, and as I did, I felt good. Actually, better than good, like a huge weight had been lifted off my chest. No more wait-and-see for me. Finally, I can say I'm done with Matt Parker.

And mean it.

Dancers are made, not born.

—*Mikhail Baryshnikov*

Monday, November 24, 7:07 a.m.
In bed

Mom left this morning to go to Atlanta, Georgia. "I'll be back Wednesday in time for the dance show," she said when she came into my room to tell me good-bye. The she bent down and kissed me. "Hold down the fort while I'm gone."

"No problem," I said. What could possibly happen in Faraway, Alabama, in two days?

8:32 p.m.
In the bathtub
OMG!

I can't believe what happened in dress
rehearsal today. Emily, who was supposed
to do the freshman solo in the dance show
Wednesday night, was going through her
routine, did a leap, landed wrong on her ankle,
and couldn't stand up. Ms. Baumann called
the school nurse, who came to take a look. She
poked, prodded, determined it was sprained
and wrapped an ice pack around it until Emily's
mom came to get her.

"Poor Emily," said Kate.

"Yeah, it's horrible." I said. All I could
think about was how excited Emily had been
to perform her jazz solo. I never thought
about what the fact that she couldn't dance
meant for the show.

"April, you'll be filling in for Emily," said
Ms. Baumann after Emily's mom left with
her. "You have two days to learn the dance,
and I have no doubt you can do it." Then she

pointed to Mady and Bree who are co-captains of the team. "Girls, you're in charge of helping April with the dance. Emily can help out from the sidelines tomorrow."

Then she motioned toward a corner of the auditorium. "Get busy," she said to the three of us. She obviously wanted us to get on it pronto.

But I was too stunned to move. Emily knew her solo perfectly. Even though she's only a freshman, she's one of the best dancers on the team. Everyone was counting on her dance to be one of the best in the show. I don't want to mess this up and let everyone on the team down.

The other freshman girls on the team crowded around me. I think they knew I needed moral support. "Oh my God, April! You're doing a solo!" said Vanessa, like the excitement of performing by myself on stage should trump the fear of doing it or the amount of work ahead of me.

"You can do it," said Kate.

I looked at Brynn. She nodded like she agreed with Kate. "You're going to be great," she said. "You're a really good dancer, April."

I know she was putting aside our differences of late to be encouraging, and it meant a lot. It was almost like getting one of the notes she used to write to me in elementary school that she used to always sign LYLAS (*Luv ya like a sister*). She was being the best friend I needed, loved, and missed.

I took a deep breath as I joined Mady and Bree, who were already waiting for me to get started. We worked on the dance for the rest of dress rehearsal, and then Ms. Baumann stayed and worked with me for a long time after everyone else left. "You're getting there," she said.

On the way home from the auditorium, the beats from the piece I'm dancing to played like a loop in my head. Interspersed with the notes were Natasha's wise words from the end of yoga class. *Each day is a new opportunity. The unexpected can happen. Embrace it.*

Today was Exhibit A, and I'm trying. Really trying.

Talked to Mom

As soon as I got out of the bathtub, I called Mom. She was so excited when I told her about the solo. "I'm very proud of you!" she said.

"You better wait until Wednesday to say that." Then I told Mom that I was pretty nervous about filling in for Emily.

"I know you'll do a great job," said Mom. "April, I'm sorry I'm in Atlanta and not at home." Her voice sounded sad. "I feel bad I can't be there when you have so much going on."

"It's OK." I didn't want it to weigh her down. She has just as much going on as I do.

"Love you, honey. More than you know."

"Love you too, Mom."

9:49 p.m.
Talked to Sophie and Leo

When I hung up with Mom, I called Sophie. She made a long *squeeee* sound into the phone when I told her about the solo.

"What was that?" I asked, laughing.

"I'm so happy for you!" she said. "I can't wait to see you dance."

One of the things I like best about Sophie is her enthusiasm. Knowing she'll be there the night of the show made me feel really good, but there was someone else I wanted to be sure would be there too. I hung up with Sophie and called Leo.

When he picked up, I told him about my solo. "It's a little scary," I admitted. "I can't imagine what it will be like to dance by myself in front of so many people."

"If this is an invitation, you might want to reconsider," said Leo. "I'm not the best dancer."

"Huh?" I was confused.

"You're inviting me to dance with you, right?" said Leo. "Like a duet."

"I want you to come to the show, not dance with me!"

Leo laughed. "Of course I'll be there. I was just teasing you."

"Oh," I said. Sometimes Leo's humor goes right by me. He can be so weird and goofy. "Are you sure you want to come?" I asked.

Leo stopped laughing. "I wouldn't want to be anywhere else."

Tuesday, November 25, 10:02 p.m.
Longest. Day. Ever.

All I did today, besides go to class and eat, was dance. Ms. Baumann met me in the gym before school and during my free period to work on my solo. Emily came to practice to help coach me through it. "You got it," she said after I'd done it for what felt like the hundredth time.

I sure hope so. The dance show is tomorrow.

Wednesday, November 26, 5:05 p.m.
Good news!

"I sold my line!" Mom said as soon as she walked into the house. She just got home from Atlanta (which is a good thing because I have to be at the auditorium at 6:00 p.m.). It was obvious Dad had already heard because he and Mom exchanged happy looks, but it was news to May and June and me. We all hugged her. "Mom, that's so great!" I said.

She smiled at me. "We'll have plenty of time to talk about it later," she said. "But right now you have a show to get to." Then Mom led me back to my bathroom and brushed my hair into a high ponytail and coiled it around into a bun. "Ready?" she asked.

I nodded.

Off I go.

10:32 p.m.
Post-show

Tonight was unforgettable in so many ways.

When I got to the auditorium, I was so nervous. I tried to calm myself down by thinking about Leo and Sophie and all the people who would be there silently cheering me on. I thought about some of the things Natasha had said at yoga, and I even tried her deep-breathing technique. I knew I was prepared, but as the sounds of the packed auditorium drifted backstage, my stomach was in free-fall mode. I thought it might drop out of my body.

Walking out on stage when the show started and doing the opening dance with the rest of the team was a blur. My jazz solo was the sixth dance in the lineup, and as each of the dances before it finished, I felt myself getting more and more nervous. When it was my turn, Ms. Baumann mouthed for to me to go. Emily was watching the show from the wings, and she squeezed my hand. As I walked onstage, I looked out into the audience, and I remember thinking that the lights were blindingly bright and I was glad I couldn't make out individual faces. I silently went over the advice Emily had given me earlier today. *Smile. Focus on each step. Dance like no one is watching.*

Then the music started, and I focused on the dance. Jump. Hitch kick. Chassé. Split leap. Double pirouette. Step after step until I'd finished.

When I was done, I heard applause. I couldn't believe I'd done it. I saw Ms. Baumann signaling for me to curtsy. "Good job," she mouthed as I walked off stage. I think she was actually smiling. Emily hugged me. So did Brynn. I was relaxed and happy as I danced the freshman group dance and then the finale with the rest of the team.

After the show, we had a party. There were flowers for Ms. Baumann and the team captains and a big cake for everyone. Parents, teachers, and friends all gathered in the lobby outside the auditorium to congratulate us. Mom, Dad, May, and June were there. And of course Gaga and Willy. Sophie stayed and so did Harry. They all told me I did a great job. Even Harry said I was "*surprisingly decent.*"

All their compliments made me feel fantastic, but the best one was from Leo. "You looked hot on stage," he said quietly. It sounded odd coming out of his mouth, and I told him so.

Leo laughed. "Actually, I've only ever used the word *hot* in connection to a Bunsen burner or soup, but you've redefined the meaning of it for me."

I'm so not hot. But I loved hearing it.

I loved the whole night.

11:12 p.m.

When we got home from the auditorium, my family had a victory party in the kitchen. "We have a lot to celebrate," said Dad as he whipped up a delicious pot of homemade hot chocolate with marshmallows.

"April, you were a star," he said.

"Yeah," said May. "I wish I could dance like that."

"You're good at so many sports," I said.

"I'm not good at sports or dancing," said June.

"But you're so smart and doing so well in school." I knew this was sounding more like a pep talk than a victory party, but I wanted my sisters to feel as good as I did. I was so relieved knowing I'd done a good job at the dance show, and it was nice sitting at the kitchen table drinking hot chocolate with my family.

It was especially nice when Dad raised his mug. "I'd like to propose a toast," he said.

"Can you do that with hot chocolate?" I asked.

"Why not?" Dad winked at me. Then he cleared his throat. "April, we're all so proud of you. You were a star tonight. All your hard work showed. Excellent job."

"Thanks, Dad." Even though he sounded

like he'd taken the script straight out of a parenting handbook, it was nice to hear.

Then he looked at Mom. "Flora, congratulations on selling your line. You know I was skeptical when you first told me you wanted to open the store." He paused. "I apologize for not supporting you 100 percent. I should have known what a success you would be."

Mom smiled at Dad. "I never expected this," she said. I knew she was talking about selling her line to the store in Atlanta, but I could totally relate to what she was saying.

When I started high school, I wasn't sure what to expect. So many things, both good and bad, happened. I guess what I've learned is that it's kind of a waste of time to have expectations of what things will be like. It's more important to just be.

Dad reached across the table and took Mom's hand in his. Then his eyes filled with tears. "You've accomplished so very much, and I'm so proud of you."

Mom was teary-eyed too as she squeezed Dad's hand.

"Why are you both crying?" asked June.

"Happy times call for happy tears," said Mom.

Mom sounded so corny, like she was in a commercial for Kleenex. But as she wiped her eyes, the truth is, I knew exactly what she meant.

The greatest secrets are always hidden in the most unlikely places.

—*Roald Dahl*

Thanksgiving, 8:02 p.m.
Home from the diner

Today my family congregated at the diner to celebrate Thanksgiving. Gaga asked Dad if she and Willy could do the cooking. Dad agreed, but only because Gaga made a huge deal about how Dad could use a break and that she and Willy had a big surprise in store for us all.

It turned out what they had in mind was more shock than surprise. Gaga and Willy cooked a vegan Thanksgiving feast. When everyone got to the diner, Gaga announced that in honor of their first anniversary (which doesn't even happen for another five weeks), she and Willy are going vegan. "That means no meat, poultry, dairy, eggs, and a few other things I can't remember at the moment," said Gaga.

What I can remember is what we had for Thanksgiving lunch: sliced tofu loaf instead of turkey, quinoa and sprouted onion stuffing, sweet potatoes topped with chopped pecans (no minimarshmallows in sight), an array of unrecognizable side dishes, gluten-free dinner rolls, and raw pumpkin pie.

When Willy brought out the pie, everyone got excited. It looked delicious, especially after what we'd had for lunch. But looks can be deceiving. When Uncle Dusty took a bite, he spit it into his napkin and downed a full glass of water. "What the heck is this?" he asked, like what he'd tasted in no way resembled any kind of pie he'd ever eaten.

"It's pumpkin pie with pumpkin, tofu, agave nectar, coconut oil, and a raw walnut crust," said Willy. Then he told us he made it from a YouTube video. He smiled like he was proud of his high-tech accomplishment. I could tell Gaga was too. She put her arm around Willy and kissed him on the lips, right in front of everybody.

I thought the kiss would be quick—after all they're both in their eighties. But octogenarians can be surprising. As they kissed, Willy wrapped his arms around Gaga, and they stayed lock-lipped for a long time. I hate to write this, but it was quite a passionate embrace.

"Is it safe for old people to kiss like that?" asked June.

"I'm going to vomit," said Harry.

"Because of the kiss or the food?" asked May.

"Both," said Amanda.

"I heard when you kiss like that you get the flu," said Charlotte.

"Or chicken pox," said Izzy.

My little cousin, Sam, covered his eyes like he didn't want to watch, which made Charlotte and Izzy do the same thing.

Aunt Lila cleared her throat. "Mom, that's enough." But I guess Gaga didn't hear her (a real possibility) or chose to ignore her (also a real possibility, which I can't blame her for), because they kept right on kissing like no one else was in the room.

All the little kids started cracking up. Gaga and Willy stopped kissing when they heard all the commotion around them. "Happy Thanksgiving!" said Gaga. She grinned at Willy who put his arms up in the air and made a victory sign like he was a quarterback who'd just thrown the winning pass.

"I guess he's happy he's still getting some at his age," Harry said to me.

"Ew!" I said. I didn't want to think about that. But it was classic Harry. Some things never change.

But some things are less predictable, like what Gaga did when she and Willy finished kissing. I thought for sure when she raised her glass, she was going to make one of her infamous toasts. But what she said really surprised me. "I'm getting old," said Gaga.

"Mom, don't be dramatic," said Aunt Lilly.

Gaga raised a brow. "I'm not being dramatic, I'm being honest. I'm too old to keep making speeches every time there's a family get-together. It's time for someone else to do it. Volunteers?"

No one moved. I think everyone was too shocked. As much as we all roll our eyes every time Gaga gets up to speak, I think the idea of her getting old and not doing it was a whole lot less palatable. Plus, I couldn't imagine who could possibly replace her.

Gaga waited for a hand to go up, but none did. "If no one is going to step up to the plate, we're going to go around the room and everyone can say what they're thankful for this Thanksgiving."

Uncle Dusty looked at his watch. I knew that meant he was ready to get this over with and go home. "I'm thankful for the delicious meal we just had," he said.

"You almost puked when you ate the pie," said Harry. Uncle Dusty ignored his son's comment and nodded at Uncle Drew like it was his turn.

"I'm thankful we can all be together as a family on Thanksgiving," said Uncle Drew.

Gaga smiled at his response, and then she motioned to Aunt Lila who went next. As Gaga continued around the room and everyone said what they were thankful for, I stopped listening and started thinking about what I was going to say when it was my turn.

There were a few things on my list.

I'm thankful Mom's store is a success and that she and Dad don't have that to fight about anymore. For that matter, I'm thankful she opened the store period. If she hadn't, I wouldn't have met Leo.

I'm thankful (shockingly) that Gaga and Willie got married. If they hadn't, I never would have met Sophie. And even though I know it's hard for her that her parents are separated and I wish it wasn't the case, I'm thankful she and her mom came to Faraway.

I'm thankful Harry and I have gotten closer. I never thought we'd hang out or that I'd think of him as a friend. He always seemed dark and moody. But he's cool and loyal. I like knowing he's on my side.

I'm thankful Brynn supported me when

she found out I was dancing the solo. I can't say it was the answer to all our troubles. But it felt nice to know, at least for the moment, that we're friends.

I'm definitely thankful I had the opportunity to dance the solo. I never dreamed I could do something like that. It's kind of cool and empowering knowing I did. Mostly, I'm just thankful I didn't screw it up.

"April, what are you thankful for?" When I heard Gaga's voice say my name, I snapped to it. Only problem: I wasn't sure what I wanted to say.

"April."

I knew everyone was waiting on me. I decided to speak the truth.

"It's kind of a hard question to answer," I said. "There are a lot of things I'm thankful for, and I can't pick just one."

When I said that, Gaga looked at Willy and they both clapped. "What a fabulous answer," said Gaga. Then she picked up a shopping bag and walked to where I was standing.

"The future of family toasting is in your

capable hands," she said to me. She pulled out a neon green T-shirt with the words FAMILY TOASTMASTER on the front and handed it to me. "Put it on," she said.

"Gaga, this is weird," I whispered in her ear. But she ignored my comment and tapped her foot like she was waiting for me to put on the shirt.

"April, this was a contest and you won," she said once I'd slipped the T-shirt on over my sweater. Then she leaned over and pinned a blue ribbon on the front of it and asked Aunt Lilly to take our picture.

"You look like you just came from the state fair," said Harry when she was done.

"Don't wear that T-shirt outside the diner," said Amanda. "The color looks awful with your hair." Then she paused. "Maybe you should bleach it."

"The shirt or her hair?" asked Sophie. Then she threw an arm around me and started laughing, which made me laugh too.

It had a chain-reaction effect that rippled across the room. Pretty soon, everyone was laughing, and I'm not even sure why. But what I am sure about is that I'm thankful for my family. They're weird and annoying and inappropriate lots of the time.

But hey, they're mine.

Ten Reasons My Life Is mostly Miserable

1. My mom: Flora.

2. My dad: Rex.

3. My little sister: May.

4. My baby sister: June.

5. My dog: Gilligan.

6. My town: Faraway, Alabama.

7. My nose: too big.

8. My butt: too small.

9. My boobs: uneven.

10. My mouth. Especially when it is talking to cute boys.

THE MOSTLY MISERABLE LIFE OF APRIL SINCLAIR

THE MOSTLY MISERABLE LIFE OF APRIL SINCLAIR

Can You Say Catastrophe?

LAURIE FRIEDMAN

THE MOSTLY MISERABLE LIFE OF APRIL SINCLAIR

Too Good to Be True

LAURIE FRIEDMAN

THE MOSTLY MISERABLE LIFE OF APRIL SINCLAIR

Truth and Kisses

LET'S KISS
FRIENDS 4EVER
TOO SOON
MAYBE NOT

LAURIE FRIEDMAN

THE MOSTLY MISERABLE LIFE OF APRIL SINCLAIR

Love or Something Like It

LAURIE FRIEDMAN

THE MOSTLY MISERABLE LIFE OF APRIL SINCLAIR

Not What I Expected

LAURIE FRIEDMAN

THE MOSTLY MISERABLE LIFE OF APRIL SINCLAIR

Too Much Drama by New Year

LAURIE FRIEDMAN

About the Author

Laurie Friedman clearly remembers her first day of high school, when her dad wouldn't allow her at the breakfast table with hot rollers in her hair. She was certain that starting one of the most important phases of her life with bad hair was a terrible sign of things to come. As it turned out, high school was filled with lots of good days—and some bad—that had absolutely nothing to do with her hair.

Laurie Friedman is the author of the Mostly Miserable Life of April Sinclair series as well as the popular Mallory series and many picture books, most recently *Ruby Valentine and the Sweet Surprise* and *Birthday Rules*. A native Arkansan, she now lives in Miami, Florida, with her family and her adorable rescue dog, Riley. She visits schools around the country to talk to students about her books and to conduct writing workshops. You can find Laurie B. Friedman on Facebook or visit her on the web at www.lauriebfriedman.com.